Tip leaned forward and took her hands in his.

"So, Kathleen Kerry Sullivan, attorney-at-law. What's the verdict? Does this change anything between us or can we pick up where we left off?"

Kerry looked at him. "I honestly don't know, Tip. All this happened so fast and so differently from the way I'd imagined it would."

Tip grinned. "You really were planning to read me the riot act, weren't you?"

Kerry had to grin back. "I was planning to prosecute to the full extent of the law."

"And now?"

"Now I don't know. I feel torn...."

He nodded. "When it happens between us," he said gently, "I want it to be complete. No doubts. No indecisions."

Kerry felt her stomach drop at the sensual promise his words held. "What makes you so sure it is going to happen?" she asked, her voice slightly hoarsened from wishing it would.

Dear Reader:

Romance offers us all so much. It makes us "walk on sunshine." It gives us hope. It takes us out of our own lives, encouraging us to reach out to others. Janet Dailey is fond of saying that romance is a state of mind, that it could happen anywhere. Yet nowhere does romance seem to be as good as when it happens *here*.

Starting in February 1986, Silhouette Special Edition is featuring the AMERICAN TRIBUTE—a tribute to America, where romance has never been so wonderful. For six consecutive months, one out of every six Special Editions will be an episode in the AMERICAN TRIBUTE, a portrait of the lives of six women, all from Oklahoma. Look for the first book, *Love's Haunting Refrain* by Ada Steward, as well as stories by other favorites—Jeanne Stephens, Gena Dalton, Elaine Camp and Renee Roszel. You'll know the AMERICAN TRIBUTE by its patriotic stripe under the Silhouette Special Edition border.

AMERICAN TRIBUTE—six women, six stories, starting in February.

AMERICAN TRIBUTE—one of the reasons Silhouette Special Edition is just that—Special.

The Editors at Silhouette Books

JILLIAN BLAKE
Sullivan vs. Sullivan

Silhouette Special Edition

Published by Silhouette Books New York

America's Publisher of Contemporary Romance

SILHOUETTE BOOKS
300 East 42nd St., New York, N.Y. 10017

Copyright © 1986 by Jillian Blake

ISBN: 0-373-09323-3

First Silhouette Books printing July 1986

America's Publisher of Contemporary Romance

Printed in the U.S.A.

Books by Jillian Blake

Silhouette Intimate Moments

Diana's Folly #27
East Side, West Side #67

Silhouette Special Edition

Water Dancer #256
Heatstroke #299
Sullivan vs. Sullivan #323

JILLIAN BLAKE

is a voracious consumer of all types of fiction from the ridiculous to the sublime. Lately, it seems she's been finding something to write about in everything she sees and does.

An ex-dancer with a five year old daughter and a husband who is a dedicated jazz musician, Jillian leads a busy and happy life in Cambridge, Massachusetts.

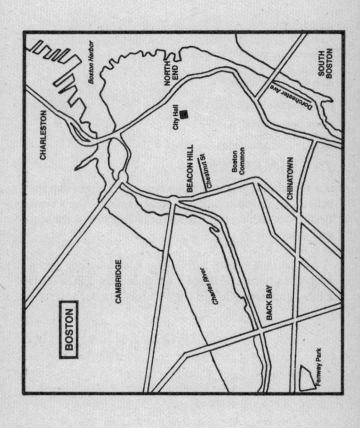

Chapter One

Dorchester Avenue was scorching hot under the August sun. The sidewalks seemed to heave under the heat and the asphalt was pebbled with sweat.

All along the Avenue, stores were shut tight against the relentless weather. The Avenue Minit Convenience Store and Marie C's Salon d'Beauté had pulled their metal shutters down against the glare but remained open to a desultory clientele. The yellow transparent plastic covering Bob the Greengrocer's windows bathed the limp produce in a lurid glow. Only the Gaelic Pub, thick-walled and windowless, seemed to be operating under a business-as-usual policy.

In the storefront offices of Sullivan and Sullivan, Attorneys-At-Law, there was no such protection against the elements. Old green shades weakly attempted to battle the relentless glare but failed. The office air conditioner, wedged into the valance over the door, was effective only if one sat directly beneath it and absorbed the drops of icy water it released every few seconds in a limp rhythm.

Kathleen Kerry Sullivan, the only inhabitant of the office was not, at that moment, pleased with her life. While most of her acquaintances enjoyed breezy vacations on Cape Cod or worked in svelte high-rise offices in downtown Boston, she was stuck on the sweltering Avenue with no relief in sight. True, the situation was entirely of her own making and Kerry rarely succumbed to self-pity. Usually she was proud of her close association with the tight-knit working-class "family" of her adopted neighborhood and looked out on the Avenue with proprietary fondness. Usually she was more resilient and had a lot more optimisim about her career and her choice to practice law in Dorchester instead of someplace more glamorous, like a big firm downtown.

But the heat had wilted her high-mindedness along with her high spirits, and just now she saw no glory in the bald realities of life that had resulted in her current uncomfortable situation. There was no glory, for instance, in having to work one's way through Suffolk Law School because Harvard had not offered a scholarship. And there was no glamour to be found this day in her connection with the penurious firm of Sullivan and Sullivan, where she had worked as a clerk all through law school, and where, after having graduated one year ago, she had found herself morally obligated to "join the firm," as old Tom Sullivan grandly put it. Morally obligated even though she was not one of the Sullivans whose name appeared on the flaking wooden sign that hung over the door.

"Old" Tom was Thomas J. Sullivan Sr., a jovial, rotund fellow in his sixties who seemed to end up handling every charity case on the Avenue despite the fact that his shirts were threadbare and the pencils on the desks mere stubs. And the salary he paid her! Well, Kerry reminded herself morosely, she wouldn't put up with it for a minute if she didn't love the old man so much. At the moment, however, her affection for him was overshadowed by a slight resentment. After all, Tom was busy "consulting with clients" in the dim coolness of the Gaelic Pub while Kerry was definitely not cooling her heels in the overheated office, but was reading a brief about an upcoming petty larceny case that she knew would mean a lot of work and little remuneration.

Not that life didn't have its rewards, although she was hard put to remember them just now. She had to remind herself, for instance, that she usually loved her job, especially when it meant eking out a morsel of justice for some penurious client who was more confused than guilty. Such was the case with Billy Stuart, whose file she now held sightlessly before her on the desk. Billy was a handyman who had drifted around the neighborhood all his life, repeating grades in school until they had graduated him more out of exasperation than out of any confidence that he could read or write. Billy was not bad, just muddled and when Mrs. Louise Ranieri accused him of stealing a television from her house while he was repairing her front steps, he had come to old Tom in befuddlement.

"I never even went into the house," he had told Tom and Kerry, more puzzled than angry. "The lady told me I had to use the gas station on the corner if I needed to...you know." He had blushed, unable to meet Kerry's eyes.

"That sounds like old Louise," Tom had muttered. "Kerry, see what you can dig up for Billy here. I've got a meeting across the street that won't wait." And Tom had left for the Gaelic, leaving Kerry to spend two hours trying to get Billy's story to make some sense.

Normally she would have had no trouble working up enthusiasm for a case like this. During her undergraduate days Kerry had been politically active, considered a "radical" by some of her friends, even though the most radical thing she had ever done was to protest the male-only policy of the law review board by writing a letter that was printed in the *Suffolk Bulletin*. Nevertheless, she had always seen herself as a true "people's lawyer," defending the underprivileged and underappreciated against the overprotected and the overfed. And she found deep satisfaction in working within the system to bring off her goals, arguing a point of law with a prosecutor and sometimes—not often, but often enough—gaining her hard-earned point and her client's victory.

With Billy Stuart, it would be hard. Mrs. Ranieri was pressing full charges against the young man, and Kerry knew the burden of proof lay in her hands, not those of the junior prosecutor who would handle the case for the plaintiff. And today, with Kerry's current mood of discomfort and rebellion, it was harder than usual to force herself to focus on what course of action would be best to take. She felt stymied and overwhelmed, and her thoughts kept drifting longingly to an air-conditioned movie theater or a breezy beach when they should have remained firmly on the case.

"Ah, Kerry, my girl, still at it?" Tom walked into the office bringing a gust of even hotter street air behind him. "Made any headway?"

Kerry looked up glumly. Tom wore a genial smile and a rumpled gray polyester suit, with his tie loosened below his ruddy face. Tom was always ruddy, so it was hard to tell whether he was red from the heat or from the several beers he had probably downed in the course of his meeting.

"I'm not sure what I can make out of Billy's statement, Tom," she reported, waving her hands over the scrawled pages of yellow legal paper with resignation. "It's hard enough to make sense out of him anyway, and I haven't gotten Mrs. Ranieri's statement yet from the district attorney's office."

Tom sat heavily in his squeaky wooden recliner and tipped it back precariously. "Old Louise won't tell you much that she doesn't want to tell," he said, lighting up one of his incessant cigars. Kerry sighed. Cigar smoke was not going to improve the air quality in the office at all. "But I can tell you to look for Mr. Ranieri to play a bit of a role in these shenanigans. That's for sure."

"Mr. Ranieri?"

"Right you are. Old Louise kicked him out a couple of days ago, according to Bobby Shea over at the pub. Said Louise was tired of his drinking and loafing and told him to get packing. So John's holed himself up in a boarding house on Avenue A with nothing to do and nothing to do it with.'' He tapped the side of his veined bulbous nose in a familiar gesture. ''My guess is he helped himself to the television to tide him over until old Louise cools off.''

For the first time that day, Kerry brightened. ''So if I can get anything pointing to the fact that John was in the neighborhood at the time, I can probably get Billy off the hook?''

Tom pursed his lips. ''I'd say you'll have a better chance than you would without such testimony. And I'd say a trip to old Louise's neighbor, Miss Carpenter, might pay off pretty well. She's a notorious busybody and there's no love lost between her and old Louise.''

Kerry grinned. She sometimes forgot that Tom, in addition to knowing more about his neighborhood than anyone else in the area, was a crafty lawyer to boot. She had seen him work magic in courtrooms when assistant DA's had smirkingly assumed that he was just another small-time shyster past his prime— seen him come alive and decimate the prosecution's case and the prosecutor along with it. Her heart swelled with fondness. He was a wonderful lawyer and a good friend.

''Oops! Almost forgot.'' Tom reached into one commodious pocket of his jacket and pulled out a frosted mug filled with partially melted ice. From the other pocket emerged a bottle of root beer. Kerry had not noticed the dark moisture stains on both sides of the jacket since Tom rarely bothered to change suits more than once a week. ''This is for you from Bobby Shea.''

"Bobby Shea, huh?" Kerry reached across for the cool glass and bottle, and held them against her forehead briefly before uncapping the root beer and pouring it into the mug. "If Bobby had sent over anything, it would have been a real beer," she chided him. "He's always trying to get me drunk. This looks more like your work, you old fox."

Tom clucked his tongue disapprovingly. "I'll have to talk to Bobby about that," he said. "It's not seemly for a young lady to be drinking in public." He frowned. "And even worse for a bartender to be aidin' and abettin' such nonsense. You're not sweet on him, are you, now?"

Kerry giggled, letting the sweet icy root beer dribble down her throat. Tom was notoriously patronizing when it came to Kerry's private life. He saw himself as something between a father figure and a parish priest, and was always trying to arrange things as he saw best and always trying to ferret out any information that might be beyond his control.

"Not to worry, Tom. I can take care of myself where Bobby is concerned."

Tom scowled, then brightened. "Hey, have you seen the latest?" He shuffled through his pockets and produced a folded sheet of newsprint, slightly damp from its contact with the root beer. "Get a load of what my boy's just pulled off. It's all right here on page twelve of the *Boston Globe*."

Kerry tried to look enthusiastic as Tom passed her the paper, but the truth was that she was tired of hearing about the latest triumphs of Thomas P. Sullivan Jr., Tom's twenty-six-year-old only son. Ever since she had begun working for Tom, she had been subjected to what she privately called the Doting Daddy Hour—short but all-too-frequent exhibitions when Tom would pull out clippings and insist on regaling Kerry with the minute details of his son's glamorous and meteoric career.

Thomas Sullivan Jr., known affectionately to everyone on the Avenue as Tip, since Tip O'Neill was a particular idol of Tom Senior's, was the other Sullivan, for whom the Sullivan and Sullivan sign waited in faded patience over the door. Tip was more than the favorite son—he was the golden boy of Dorchester Avenue, their great hope and claim to fame. If Tom didn't show Kerry the latest clipping containing mention of the great Tip—something which had never happened and was not likely to—then Kerry was certain to come across it pinned up in the Avenue Convenience Store or even in Marie's.

Tip had graduated from Harvard Law School a year before and had gone right into the state attorney general's office as an assistant district attorney. Right from the start, it seemed that Tip was given important state-level cases to handle; he never had to go through an apprenticeship plowing through low-level city cases like the rest of the staff had do do. He seemed to have a penchant for involving himself in the kinds of cases Kerry was most interested in, cases involving the kinds of criminals and con men who often wound up victimizing her clients on Dorchester Avenue. He had already been instrumental in gathering evidence that had resulted in the indictment of the top people in one of the biggest loan-shark operations that had been plaguing the area, and after only five months on the job, he had stood in for an ailing senior DA and prosecuted a big case involving laundered betting funds in the North End.

Still, despite her interest in his work, Kerry had to force herself to read Tip's press. One of the reasons, she readily admitted to herself, was pure jealousy. Tip's was a plum job, for which Kerry would gladly have given her eye teeth had there been a chance in hell that she could get it. But jobs like Tip's were offered only to the best and the brightest, and even then usually because someone like Tom had labored long and hard to pave the way. Kerry had graduated at the top of her class at Suffolk, but Suffolk wasn't Harvard, and anyway, she was the wrong Sullivan in a town where the name meant a lot. Her family came from New Jersey, not South Boston, and at the State House on Beacon Hill, the New Jersey Sullivans carried little weight.

The strangest thing was that Kerry had never even met Tip. The closest she'd ever come was in reading his acclaimed entries in the *Harvard Law Review*, at Tom's insistence—she had to admit they were pretty good—and in exclaiming politely over dim photographs of him such as the one Tom waved before her now. "What's he done?" she asked with what she hoped sounded like genuine interest. "Cracked the local Mafia connection singlehandedly?"

"No, no, no. I mean, he's probably working on that, but this is something very different. Look. See? There he is. Right there, at a Kennedy family picnic down there in Hyannisport. See him? He's practically standing right next to Ted Kennedy!"

Kerry looked closely. An additional frustration of the Doting Daddy shows was the fact that Tip's picture was always dim and blurry, and he was often lost in a crowd as he was in the fuzzy black-and-white before her now. She could make out Senator Kennedy and a few other familiar-looking faces, but she could not see anything that remotely resembled Tip Sullivan. "I can't..." she began, but Tom impatiently took the photo out of her hand.

"Look. Right there. See? There's his head and his shoulder and...there, you can see his face, or most of it anyway, sticking right out behind the Senator's."

Now Kerry saw what he was pointing to. Far back in the crowd stood a tallish man with tousled hair and a nicely squared jaw. He was wearing the regulation polo shirt and chinos and, as far as Kerry could tell, looked pretty much like the rest of the men in the photo—healthy, preppy and confident in his summer tan. But Kerry thought she saw a certain twinkle in the one eye that was available to the camera, a twinkle that seemed to say, "Do you believe this is all for real? I don't."

But of course it was impossible to tell for sure. And Kerry didn't think that Tip Sullivan was capable of that sort of self-irony. That would have been a redeeming quality, and the truth was she didn't like Tip much. Part of her reason was personal: Tom always joked that he had hired Kerry because of her last name, so that he could make her a full partner on the letterhead if not in salary, but Kerry knew that he would have only minimal regrets at bumping her back to associate, or even out the door altogether, when and if his son Tip made his prodigal return to the family firm.

"When Tip comes to work here," Tom would say, a bemused smile on his face, "things are gonna be different, I can tell you that, Kerry. We're gonna get the kind of cases in here we've always dreamed of handling, you know what I mean? I mean the big ones, the ones that really matter."

"What we do matters, Tom," Kerry would say gently, unwilling to burst his balloon of dreams. "It matters a lot to the people we help. You know that."

Tom waved his hands impatiently in the air. "I know. I know. And we'll keep on taking care of family, sure! But with Tip's experience, and with his connections in the attorney general's office, well, by the time he's ready to come home and set up shop with me here, he'll be just about the biggest name in law in this town. Bigger than F. Lee Bailey. Heck, some day he may be just like his namesake in Washington!" Tom had met Tip O'Neill a few times in his life, and considered him a friend as well as a political idol.

Kerry would sigh and agree, simply because she could not bear to do otherwise. But the truth was— and this was the other, larger reason for her instinctive dislike of Tip Sullivan—that she had an awful suspicion that old Tom waited in vain. Tip, she believed, had no intention of honoring the partnership that had been waiting for him ever since he had been old enough to strut down the Avenue in his father's proud shadow.

And so, because she loved old Tom as fiercely as she loved the work he did, despite days like this, Kerry labored doggedly on in silence, allowing Tom his fantasies and harboring a secret resentment toward his preppy and successful son, who she feared had left the Avenue behind forever.

It wasn't all work, despite Kerry's limited budget and the long erratic hours she put in. In the late afternoon, when the sun had dipped behind the tall facade of the Sacred Heart Church and the Avenue had cooled considerably, Kerry ventured out to do a little legwork on the Billy Stuart case. She did not find Miss Carpenter at home, and Mrs. Ranieri did not answer her doorbell, but Kerry was certain she had seen the curtains pulled aside in the dining room as she stood on the porch. But a visit to Marie's Salon d'Beauté to say hello to her friend Marie Cormier paid off.

"What're you doin' loose so early in the day?" Marie asked brightly when Kerry came in. Marie stood behind a thin older woman, putting her hair in pin curls and managing to speak clearly despite a mouthful of bobby pins. "Old Tom must be slipping in the slave labor department."

Kerry made a face and slipped into the empty chair next to where Marie worked. "Ahhh, it's so cool in here," she said, leaning her head back gratefully and letting the air slip over her long neck and throat. "Actually, I'm still on the job. Out doing a little sleuthing for a new case."

"I should have known," Marie said, clicking her teeth. She was an ample woman of about thirty-four with a head full of red curls and saucy brown eyes that always seemed to hold a teasing challenge. Marie had grown up on the Avenue and knew almost as much about it as Tom, although her knowledge of the seedier side of life there seemed to stem from personal experience. She had been married three times and was currently involved with one of the habitués of the Gaelic Pub, whom Tom had described as "distasteful." But despite the difference in their backgrounds and occupations, Marie and Kerry had taken an instant liking to each other, and Marie had appointed herself Kerry's guide through the labyrinthine social network that made up the Avenue and surrounding neighborhood. "Who's done what this time?" she asked with interest. Marie always had something to say about everybody, and Kerry often bent the rules about lawyer's confidentiality in exchange for the insight Marie provided.

"A young man named Billy Stuart," Kerry said. "He's been charged with stealing something from Mrs. Ranieri's house."

"Ah, poor Billy. Always getting in over his head." Marie shook her head. Then, to her surprise, the woman on whom she was working sat forward with a jolt that left a thin gray strand of curl dangling wildly across her forehead.

"Poor Billy is right!" she declared loudly. "And this time that hag next door has gone too far!" She waved her finger threateningly in the air.

Kerry looked at her and then at Marie. "Miss Carpenter?" she mouthed questioningly.

"None other," Marie replied.

"Miss Carpenter, you're just the woman I've been looking for. My name is Kerry Sullivan and—"

"I know who you are, young lady, and I know what you're here for. You want me to tell you what happened yesterday at Louise's house to get little Billy

Stuart off the hook!'' She cackled triumphantly, and Kerry could only nod, not sure how to handle this sudden onslaught.

''Well, there's nothing I'd like better than to see Louise Ranieri made a liar. God knows she deserves it. But you can tell that boss of yours that unless he apologizes to me for what happened, I'll be no good to him or his client!'' With that she settled back fiercely in her chair.

''What...what happened?'' Kerry inquired weakly.

''Hmmph. Ask old Tom Sullivan. He'll tell you, if he dares!''

Kerry looked helplessly at Marie, who rolled her huge eyes and shrugged. ''Now, Miss C., let's get you under that drier quick so you can be home in time to watch your favorite TV show.'' She bundled the little lady out of her chair and under one of the big pink hair driers along the opposite wall. Marie returned to where Kerry sat and immediately began a vigorous brushing of her friend's short dark hair. ''Well, counselor, you certainly made quick work of that little job.''

''What on earth could Tom have done to make her so mad?'' Kerry wondered.

''I don't know. Probably didn't ask her to the prom fifty years ago or something. Elsie Carpenter doesn't forget. That's why she's wearing her hair the same way she did when she was twenty-two.''

''How do you know how she wore it when she was twenty-two?''

''Just a wild guess,'' Marie replied. ''Now, when are you going to let me do something new with your hair,

Miss Sullivan? You've probably been wearing it in the same poorboy cut since *you* were twenty-two.''

"Four years isn't so bad," Kerry pointed out. Nevertheless, she cocked her head and gazed appraisingly at her reflection in the pink-framed mirror. She had a heart-shaped face with a generous mouth and a slightly snubbed nose. Her best feature, so she had always been told, was her eyes, long and elegant and a unique pale gray flecked with dark green. Long dark lashes lay across her olive, slightly sallow skin. "I need to get out in the sun and get rid of this yellow look, that's all," she mused. "And maybe a trim in front." She tossed her hair out of her eyes, where it invariably fell. "I don't think I'm ready for a new hairdo yet, though." She grinned up at Marie who threw down the brush in mock exasperation.

"I give up. You're hopeless." She came around and sat in the chair Miss Carpenter had vacated. "So. What are you up to tonight?"

"I hadn't thought about it yet," Kerry admitted. "Want to see a movie?"

"Only if it's in an air-conditioned theater," Marie said. "I'll sit through a triple feature if it's cool."

"What about Buddy? Aren't you going to see him tonight?"

Marie scowled. "That rat? Forget it. His idea of a good time is sitting in the pub drinking with the boys and making obnoxious remarks about me in front of them."

"Marie, you don't mean it. Why do you put up with him?"

Marie rolled her eyes suggestively. "He has his assets, believe me, honey. But he's working tonight anyway, so I'm free. Whaddya wanna see?"

"Anything as long as it isn't like the last movie you took me to." Kerry shuddered at the memory of the horror movie Marie had dragged her to the previous week. She had spent most of her time curled up in the scratchy seat, staring at the gum wads stuck to the floor and listening to Marie screech delightedly at each axing.

Marie laughed. "Okay, we'll play it tame tonight. Hey, did you see the Golden Boy today?"

Kerry knew exactly what she was talking about. "What do you think? Tom's probably showed it to everyone on the Avenue by now."

"Miss Carpenter brought in this copy." Marie reached forward and lifted a cleaner copy of the same newspaper photo off the counter. She looked at it and shook her head admiringly. "You gotta admit he travels in good company."

"Oh, Marie, he was probably one of a hundred people invited to Hyannisport to pay off some political debt or something. You don't think he really pals around with the senator, do you?"

"I wouldn't put anything past our Tip," Marie replied. Despite her generally healthy attitude toward most of the Avenue's denizens, even Marie seemed to have a weak spot where Tip was concerned. "After all, he's an up-and-coming figure in the city, and the Kennedys have always kept their hand in city politics."

"Marie, Tip is a lawyer. He's not running for public office, although I'm sure the Avenue would elect him to King if he wanted.

"Not yet," Marie said, still gazing at the photo. "But I bet he goes into politics some day, and when he does . . . Boy, he does look good. He's got a real sexy smile, don't you think? Kinda makes you feel like he's winking straight at you, ya know?"

Despite the fact that she had received much the same impression, Kerry chose to deny it. "I wouldn't know. After all, I've never met the man, remember?"

"You mean he still hasn't come around to see his father?"

"Not when I've been around he hasn't. And I'm sure Tom wouldn't forget to tell me if he had."

"Now that's a shame. After all Tom has done for him, Tip should be more loyal." Marie clucked her tongue disapprovingly.

Loyalty was highly regarded on the Avenue, and Kerry understood the tremendous pain Tom must feel at his son's defection. She sighed. Only Tom's eternal optimism could be keeping him afloat in the face of Tip's obvious lack of filial devotion.

But Marie had brightened. "Well, I'll lay odds that when you finally do meet our Tip in the flesh, you'll be glad you did." She narrowed her heavily made-up eyes. "And I'd even lay odds that you two might get it on like nobody's business." She gazed with frank admiration at Kerry's slim figure. "I'll bet Tip wouldn't mind a piece of that," she added frankly.

Kerry was used to Marie's coarse manner of speaking. "The only thing Tip Sullivan will get from me, when and if we do ever meet, is a piece of my mind. I think he's a real jerk to abandon his father like that. The least he could do is visit every once in a while. Even a phone call would do the trick."

"You can't get it on over the phone," Marie observed mischievously, and Kerry decided it was time the subject of Tip Sullivan was put to rest.

Chapter Two

Kerry and Marie went to see an outer space, sci-fi extravaganza at one of the big movie houses near the Boston Common, and it turned out to be an excellent choice. It was one of the few movies neither woman had seen in their constant quest to escape the August heat, and it provided just the right combination of thrills and fun to satisfy their diverse tastes. Kerry, whose first choice would have been a foreign film or a tear-jerking romance, was glad that she had opted for sheer escapism. Her earlier discomfort and dissatisfaction seemed to evaporate in the air-conditioned comfort of the dark theater.

When they emerged from the movie house, however, they were hit once again by the heat, which seemed to have risen up from the cracks in the sidewalk, where it had been lurking all day. Although the temperature had dropped, there was no hint of a breeze, and the humidity seeped through Kerry's cotton sundress and covered her skin like a warm wool blanket.

"God, I think it's gotten even hotter again," she complained as they crossed Tremont Street to the Boston Common.

"It's all the cement," Marie replied listlessly, fanning herself with the thin end of her clutch bag. "It holds the heat and then throws it back at you at night." She scowled. "We might be cooler on the Common, if we can handle the human nuisance factor."

Kerry knew that Marie was referring to the population of street people, many of them drunks, who inhabited the park at night, but she was willing to take the risk in order to escape the heat on the sidewalk. At least under the trees they might be able to locate a small breeze. "I just can't face the thought of going back to my apartment yet," she said as they headed down one of the paths that crisscrossed the park. "It's probably hotter than anyplace else in the city."

Marie winked. "That's what you get for wanting to live on fashionable Beacon Hill," she taunted mildly. "At least in Dorchester there's a little breathing room between the houses."

Kerry made a face. Marie was always trying to get her to move into the Avenue neighborhood, citing lower crime rates, more space and the indubitable fact that "the family would take care of you there." But Kerry enjoyed the cosmopolitan atmosphere of Boston's Beacon Hill and the sense of history that pervaded even her tiny third floor walk-up on Chestnut

Street. Also, she suspected that to move into Dorchester might mean to give over her identity entirely to the Avenue and "the family," and she wasn't sure she wanted to be swallowed whole by that aspect of her life. After all, she did have other interests, although at the moment she couldn't quite remember what they were.

It was a little cooler on the Common, and the air definitely felt cleaner. Marie and Kerry wandered along for a while until they were drawn by the sound of music drifting through the trees. It came from the direction of a marble rotunda that stood in the middle of a small stand of birches and which was raised above the surrounding grass by three stone steps and supported by pillars of slender pink marble.

Beneath it, isolated in the center by a single small spotlight, stood a musician holding a violin beneath his chin. His instrument was not amplified, but the sound was strong and clear in the still air, and it wove out through the darkness like a refreshing liquid balm. Others had drawn closer to listen, but like Kerry and Marie, they seemed content to keep a formal distance between them and the violinist, so that he seemed walled off in a pool of weak light and strong sound.

The music he played was classical, although he added a contemporary rhythmic pulse that pulled it out of the past and set people's toes tapping involuntarily. He spun through rapid arpeggios and cascaded back down into adagios with equal finesse, all the while caressing the instrument with his chin and his bow. His fingers seemed unnaturally long and slender in the oblique light, and they danced around the neck of the violin like shadows dancing around a flame.

It was obvious to Kerry that he was a gifted musician, and she wondered whether he was a moonlighting professional or an undiscovered genius. In either case, his music was cool and mesmerizing, and she closed her eyes to let it envelop her more completely.

"I don't believe it!" Kerry's bemusement was interrupted by Marie, who grabbed Kerry's arm excitedly. "I don't believe what my eyes are actually seeing. Look! Look there!"

Slightly annoyed, Kerry followed Marie's finger. "What? Where? I don't see anything."

"You don't? Don't you see? It's him! In the flesh!"

Kerry managed to find the figure that Marie was pointing to, but for some reason, she still could not fathom what Marie meant. Lolling against a straight and narrow birch tree trunk stood a tall man with dark hair, and both hands in his pockets. He seemed to be relaxed, but there was an air of poise about him, almost of readiness, as if he might take flight at a moment's notice. From what little Kerry could make out of his features, he was a man only vaguely familiar, if at all. She frowned and shook her head.

"I still don't see…" And then she knew who he was.

Tip Sullivan. In the flesh. And looking so much like his photos, even down to the slightly muted features—thanks to the darkness—that she wondered why she did not figure it out immediately.

She was silent so that she could watch him at her leisure. He was wearing a striped short-sleeved shirt that looked impossibly crisp and cool, and the regulation tan chinos. One foot was cocked over the other, so she could tell he wore loafers without socks. His hair was darker than she had imagined it to be, and longer. But his features, what she could make out of them, were exactly what she remembered from countless photographs. The only thing she couldn't read was his expression.

Before she could say a word, Marie had taken off. She crossed the rotunda behind the violinist in a few swift steps and approached Tip. From where she was standing, Kerry saw that he tensed slightly when Marie first came into his range of vision. Both hands came out of his pockets at once, and he looked quickly to either side of him before focusing on Marie. Obviously she had to introduce herself, for Kerry saw Tip bend his head forward to catch Marie's name. Then his face broke into a big smile and he grabbed Marie and gave her a hug.

She'll love that, Kerry thought dryly. She still hadn't thought about how she was going to handle an introduction if one came up, but she wouldn't have been terribly surprised if Marie had taken off with Tip without even coming back to say goodbye. Marie lived on instinct and impulse, and it wouldn't have been the first time that Kerry had been left to make her own way home.

But Marie pointed in Kerry's direction and, linking her arm through Tip's, began to make her way back across the small open space. For a moment Kerry entertained the thought of running away. Somehow, after all these months of imagining what it would be like to meet Tom's son, she didn't feel prepared for the actual event.

"Hey!" Marie called out loudly as they approached. "Look at what I found lurking under a tree!" She unlinked her arm from Tip's just enough so that he could extend his arm for a handshake. "I've found the famous Tom Sullivan Jr., better known to all of us as Tip."

"I don't know how famous I am," he said with a smile. "But the undeniable truth is that I'm Tip. How do you do?"

He looked straight into Kerry's eyes, and she was disarmed enough to smile back. "How do you do?" she responded automatically.

Marie, seeing that Kerry had made no move to introduce herself, decided to do the honors for her. "This here is Kathleen—hey!"

She jumped as Kerry's foot landed discreetly but firmly on her sandaled toe.

"I'm Kathleen," Kerry said quickly, and extended her hand forcefully in front of Tip so that his gaze was forced from Marie's puzzled face. "It's a pleasure to meet you, Tip." Although she continued to smile at Tip, she radioed a warning to Marie not to say anything. Kerry couldn't have said why she had impulsively decided not to reveal her identity or her connection with Tip's father, but having made the decision, she was determined to stick to it.

Marie, after giving Kerry a puzzled glare, retreated a step or two, leaving Kerry in charge of her own introduction. If Tip was aware of the unspoken dialogue that passed between the two women, he chose to ignore it.

"I don't remember seeing you around the Avenue," he said. "I certainly would have remembered if you had been there in my day."

Kerry nodded graciously. "I'm afraid I arrived after you moved away," she replied demurely, knowing that Marie would catch the implied sarcasm in the last phrase and wondering if Tip would.

He didn't. "That's too bad. We need more sights like you on Dorchester Avenue."

"Oh, you'd be surprised at the changes that have gone on there in the past few years."

Kerry hoped Tip wouldn't ask her to enumerate, since in fact, very little had changed in the past few decades. But Tip seemed far more interested in her than in the Avenue.

"Where do you work?" he inquired.

"I work...I'm...uh...I'm with Marie." Although this was not exactly an out and out lie, it was close enough to make Kerry stutter and Marie snicker. But again, Tip seemed oblivious to the undercurrent.

"And what did you say your last name was?"

"I didn't. Oh, look!" Kerry pointed across Tip's shoulder in the direction of the violinist, who had just been joined by a burly flutist. She intended only to take his attention off the conversation at hand, but Tip's reaction was remarkable. He whirled around and went into a semicrouch, looking quickly to his right and left, and his hand went to his pocket. It took him a moment to realize what was going on onstage, and then a moment more before he could straighten up and relax.

"What're you, playing cops and robbers?" Marie asked. She looked at Kerry and shrugged as if the entire situation was beyond her grasp.

Tip laughed easily and shook his head. "I guess that's what comes of hanging out on the Common. You get kind of jumpy."

"What *are* you doing hanging out on the Common?" Marie inquired. "I mean, just this afternoon you were hanging out with the Kennedys, according to the *Globe*, and now, well, you're...slumming."

Tip laughed again and Kerry had to admit she liked the sound. It was big and genuine and not at all affected. He also had a set of dazzling white teeth, and she couldn't help wondering what they cost old Tom in dental bills.

But Tip could choreograph a social situation as well as Kerry could, and now he took complete control, leaving the questions of his odd behavior and, fortunately, of Kerry's last name unanswered. "Look," he said, flinging a casual arm around both Kerry's and Marie's shoulders. "I've heard this flutist before, and he's not half as good as his partner there. As a matter of fact, he kind of kills the mood." He looked up at the rotunda where the flutist was, in fact, playing a less-than-captivating melody and grinned. "What do you say we repair to the nearest air-conditioned pub for a nightcap. Marie? Kathleen?"

Marie and Kerry looked at each other. "It's okay by me," Marie said at once. "I'd adore a drink."

Kerry nodded her assent. Like father, like son, she thought dryly. They crossed the Common, circled the Public Gardens and went into the Hampshire House bar.

"Hey! Isn't this the place they used for the TV series *Cheers*?" Marie inquired eagerly.

"The show was allegedly based on this pub, yes," Tip allowed. He was watching Kerry as he spoke.

How like a lawyer he sounded, she thought. And then she reminded herself that it took one to know one and that she wasn't supposed to be a lawyer tonight.

"Do you watch that show often, Kathleen?" he asked her.

"I don't watch much TV," she admitted.

"Well I do, and I love it," Marie chimed in enthusiastically. "I think that Sam fellow is God's gift. I really do." She looked around and frowned at the older man behind the bar. "You'd think they'd at least try and recapture his essence in here, don't you?"

Kerry had to laugh at Marie's irrepressible style, and they sat down at a comfortable table near the bar. The room was filled with men and women dressed like professionals and a few couples obviously on dates. There were perhaps half a dozen single men without jackets at the bar, but otherwise it could have been a corporate gathering of yuppies. Kerry sighed and wished she weren't wearing a sundress, although she knew that a suit was not her style, and even less so if she was posing as a hairdresser from Marie C's Salon. Every once in a while she got hit by the "could-have-beens" in this manner, and she had to remind herself that she really didn't care for that kind of life and wouldn't be happy if she had it.

Tip, however, was clearly at ease in this milieu despite his jacketless state. He smiled and waved at several fellow patrons, and a few of them even looked as if they might approach the table. Then they noticed his two companions, Kerry in her yellow sundress and Marie in a tight red jumpsuit and a healthy serving of eye makeup, and seemed to change their minds. Kerry reminded herself once again not to let it get to her.

"So, Tip," she said when their drinks had arrived. "What have you been doing these past few years?"

She had expected a brief, perhaps self-effacing summary of his work after leaving law school. What she got was something entirely different. Tip looked at her closely, smiled a little bit and then settled himself more comfortably in his chair. "Let's see," he began speculatively. "Shall I start from the top or just mention the high points?"

Kerry smiled thinly. The last thing she wanted was a Doting Daddy session from the prodigal's point of view. "The high points will do," she replied. She exchanged glances with Marie, who was smiling broadly at a man at the bar and not listening at all.

"I think the most interesting case was the one involving the laundered illegal betting money in Revere," Tip began, and launched into a long description of the history of the case and its principal participants. Despite her initial inclination to take everything Tip said with a grain of salt, Kerry found herself immediately drawn into the story. For one thing, Tip was an excellent raconteur, a trait he had clearly inherited from his father, and he had a terrific ear for dialogue. He managed to tell the story without emphasizing his role in it, although Kerry knew from the inevitable newspaper clippings that his role had been considerable. And he drew her in so expertly that she never realized he was using complicated legal terms without bothering to explain them to her, and she never thought to stop him and ask what they meant. The world he spoke about was exactly the kind of world Kerry would have loved to have been a part of: the dedicated staff of attorneys investigating and probing for the truth among mountains of carefully contrived evidence; the petty criminals victimized by the big businessmen who had managed to escape the law until now; and the intrigue of the superior courthouse with its jury trials and press boxes, so different from the tawdry hearing rooms in district court, where Kerry often argued her cases in front of desultory judges and lazy court stenographers.

She was clearly dazzled and sat forward with her chin resting between her two fists, her eyes gleaming with vicarious excitement as Tip spun his yarn. From there he moved on to a description of how he had arrived at the prosecution presentation he had given in place of the senior DA. He took her through the arguments clearly but without condescending, and Kerry listened raptly, nodding to indicate that she understood the legal processes he had used.

She forgot all about Marie and the Hampshire House pub. She forgot that she was supposed to be a hairdresser from Dorchester Avenue whose legal experience would most likely have stopped at a traffic ticket. Most of all, she forgot that she was sitting with Tom Sullivan's golden boy, the man whom she had come to dislike and whom she had long planned to confront with his filial disloyalty when and if they met. She was more than charmed—she was hypnotized.

"So, you see, I end up in some pretty odd situations in my line of work," Tip concluded. He, too, had leaned forward with his elbows on the table and one hand stretched out close to Kerry's slim brown arm. "With all the support I get from my colleagues, there's still something kind of isolating about my work. Sometimes it's safer to be alone."

Kerry's mind was working fast on its legal track. "Were you involved in something tonight?" she inquired.

Tip's eyes narrowed briefly, and then he smiled. "Let's just say it's not a good idea to be hanging around that rotunda unless you have to." His fingers inched closer to Kerry's arm. "Although I must admit I'm very glad you showed up tonight, Kathleen."

Kerry looked down and saw his hand. One perfectly manicured finger stretched out and gently brushed against her skin just above her crooked elbow. It moved back tentatively and then, when she made no move to change her position, returned with a more extended caress.

It was just one finger and just the skin of her elbow, but Kerry found the sensation impossible to resist and even moved her arm so that she could feel the feathery touch better. His finger was strong and flat-tipped, the nail clean and moon-shaped. She liked the way it ruffled the tiny pale hairs on her arm and the contrast between her tan and the pink of his nail.

Then something made her look up, and she caught his eyes. He was smiling at her in an odd way, half amused and half amazed. "Sometimes," he whispered, "it's better not to be alone. I'm glad to meet you, at last, Kathleen Whoever-You-Are."

His finger still toyed with the fleshy skin above her bent elbow and now even worked its way into the fold on the inside of her arm. But Kerry could not take her eyes off his face. Now is the time, she told herself. Now is the time to tell him who you really are and what you really think of him. Now is the time to mention that old Tom Sullivan would appreciate a visit or even a phone call, that he could not live on fond memories and pride forever. Now was the time to come up with all those sharp comments she had planned in private so many times before, those barbed remarks that would reveal her clever legal mind as well as her low opinion of Tip Sullivan.

But she couldn't think of a thing to say or a way to say it. Instead, she and Tip continued to stare into each other's eyes, hers searching the warm brown depths of his as if she were reading a long and complicated message there, although she could not have said what the message held for her.

They were interrupted by Marie, who cleared her throat loudly from somewhere above them. They looked up to see her standing in front of them, an amused expression on her face. "Uh, I hate to interrupt this fascinating conversation," she said with obvious relish, "but I just wanted to tell you guys goodnight."

Kerry blinked. "Good night? But...why good night?"

Marie rolled her eyes. "Well, it's been fabulous listening to your stories, but I've got to get going. It is after midnight, you know."

Kerry and Tip both checked their watches, obviously surprised. "After midnight?" Kerry half rose in her chair. "God, I had no idea. Wait. I'll leave with you."

"Leave? Who said anything about leaving? I just said good-night to you two."

Kerry didn't understand until Marie cocked her head and indicated the bar behind her. A man sat on a stool looking over his shoulder at them. He was about forty-five or fifty, heavyset, with a thick head of wavy silver hair.

"Marie." Kerry shook her head in exasperation. "You don't even *know* the guy."

Marie shrugged. "I do now. He's in TV production or something. Works on the Channel Four newscast. Knows Bobby Lobel, the sportscaster." She grinned. "What more do I need to know?"

"Don't be silly." Kerry stood up fully now and looked around for her purse. She felt as if she had just walked out of a double feature, hazy and a little bit confused. "I'll walk you to your car and then go home myself. I have to be at work early tomorrow."

"Nah. I just gave you the morning off. Me too."

Kerry put her hands on her hips and glared at Marie, who seemed to enjoy trapping Kerry in her own lie. "Marie, don't be silly!"

"Don't you be silly," Marie retorted amiably. "I just met this gentleman, and you just met Tip, so I'd say we're both in the same boat, wouldn't you?" She smiled brightly at Tip. "I guess I can count on an old friend to see that my new friend gets home safely, can't I, Tip?"

He smiled graciously and nodded. "Of course you can. but who's going to see that the same thing happens to you?"

Marie laughed. "You should know me well enough to know that I can take care of myself, Tip. Besides, at thirty-five a woman can't always be thinking about safe." She looked at Kerry and winked broadly.

"Sometimes she's gotta think about fun." And she sauntered back to the bar.

"I would say," Tip observed with a chuckle, "that your boss might have a point there. Don't you agree?"

"I don't know." Kerry was still watching the man at the bar skeptically. "Sometimes I think Marie looks for trouble." Kerry wasn't prepared to look back at Tip. Marie's defection had not only brought Kerry back to her senses but had pointed out the awkwardness of her situation, as well. The best thing to do, she knew, would be to tell Tip right then who she was, before she got in any deeper with him.

"Tip, I . . ."

"I know. You'd like to go home." Tip stood up and came around to pull out her chair for her. "I promised Marie I'd escort you home, and I'd never break a promise to Marie."

"You don't have to. I can go home alone." Having missed another opportunity, Kerry now thought it would be best if she at least escaped with her dignity. The longer she waited, the harder it got, and it might be better just to forget the entire episode.

But Tip would not hear of it. "Don't be silly. I want to walk you home. Besides, I want to hear all about your job, now that you've listened so politely to my monologue." And he gave her a deeply private smile that could have meant so many things.

Kerry took a deep breath and walked out of the bar ahead of him. The night seemed to have cooled off at last, and she thought she could detect a faint sea breeze blowing in from the east. A sea breeze meant her apartment would be bearable.

Tip fell into step beside her but made no further attempts to draw her out about her job, for which Kerry was secretly grateful. They walked down Beacon Street in companionable silence, turning up Charles Street with its old-fashioned street lamps and neat brick rows of antique shops. At Chestnut they turned again and headed up the steep incline of the Hill.

Kerry loved the Hill at night. People often asked her if it was safe there, what with the derelict population from the nearby Common seeking shelter in the many narrow alleyways that separated the houses. But regardless of the reality, Kerry always felt safe. She loved the silence in which her footsteps echoed neatly on the brick sidewalks, loved the faint scent of flowers from the myriad window boxes and tiny gardens hidden behind the steep brick walls. Several cats prowled the neighborhood faithfully each night, and she liked to think that they kept watch over their small domain.

This night, she should have been enjoying the pleasant company of the tall man at her side, but Kerry was too absorbed in her own thoughts, which were considerably less than serene. Every time she thought she had worked up the courage to confess to Tip, something stopped her. She was momentarily distracted by the ripple of a breeze through the ailanthus tree overhead, or she decided that her choice of words was too harsh or not harsh enough. Several times she even opened her mouth, but each time she shut it firmly again, cursing her sudden lack of articulateness and wondering what could possibly be standing in her way.

Tip seemed not to notice, or not to mind, either the silence or Kerry's preoccupation. He simply strolled

along beside her, occasionally looking up at a particularly fetching window arrangement or ornately
carved doorway. He was so casual, in fact, that Kerry
couldn't remember when he had taken her arm and
lightly looped it through his. She also realized, too
late, that the gentle pressure of his side against her
shoulder was a definite factor in her inability to speak.
Simply put, she was enjoying herself too much to want
to ruin it.

By the time they reached her front step, a narrow
entryway with a bright red door, Kerry knew there was
only one thing she could possibly say: "Come in."

She unlocked the door and they climbed the three
sets of narrow, curving stairs to her apartment at the
top of the building. As she had hoped, the three small
rooms had cooled down considerably, and she could
even see the curtains in her bedroom lifting on the
night breeze.

Tip walked right over to the desk in her living room
and switched on the lamp, which shed a soft pink glow
through its shell glass shade. He then moved with
perfect authority to the bowfront windows, pushed
back the curtains and opened the windows still further. He leaned out and looked around before turning around to face her.

"A nice view," he observed. "Both inside and out."

Kerry looked around. The living room was small
and sparsely furnished with a soft old love seat and a
deep, wing chair. A tiny mock oriental rug lay beneath the steamer trunk that served as a coffee table
and several unframed prints adorned the deep peach-
colored walls. Her dining room table stood behind the
sofa and her desk, littered with books and papers,

against the only vacant wall. It was not exactly a dream house, but she was attached to it, and she was glad that there was no condescension or falseness in Tip's voice.

"I love my little attic space," she agreed. "It's small, but it's all I need." Then she followed his eyes and saw that he was looking at the law books that were spread across her desk. Okay, she told herself with a sinking heart. The moment of truth has arrived without my help.

"Somebody around here studying law?" Tip asked, his eyebrows arched high in an expression she found strongly reminiscent of his father.

"Well, uh..." She took a deep breath. "I am. I mean, I did." She waited for him to demand an explanation.

Instead, Tip just smiled and crossed the room. "Good," he said softly, gathering her in his arms. "I just wanted to make sure there was no rival for my affections on the premises."

And with that, he pressed his mouth against hers in a long, deep and hungry kiss.

If Kerry had had any idea that she would be better able to reveal her identity to Tip in her apartment, she knew at that moment that she had been lying to herself all along. This was what she wanted, to feel those strong arms wrapped around her back so that the flat-tipped fingers practically touched the edges of her breasts on the opposite sides; to feel his torso pressing against her, the metal clip of his belt jutting out slightly into her ribcage, his thighs pressing hers back; to smell his clean scent and feel the cool smoothness of his cheek and the warm hardness of his teeth through his lips. She responded automatically by opening her lips slightly and lifting her arms around his neck. The back of his hair prickled her forearms gently and she pressed her small breasts against him so that she could feel his heart and he hers. She was quite sure that this was the right thing to do—after all, it felt so good. She thought briefly of Marie and smiled inwardly.

Tip took a step back and lowered them both to the love seat. Kerry sat half on an opened law review book, but she didn't mind. Tip's mouth was open now, his tongue pressing against hers and then darting out to shower her face with quick little rainfalls of kisses. His arms pulled her even closer against him and he leaned back against the arm of the love seat, pulling her against him so that her body could stretch sinuously along his.

"I don't want you to think," he murmured after a while as his mouth travelled through her short hair to her ear, "that I do this sort of thing all the time."

Kerry chuckled against his neck. "Isn't that supposed to be my line?"

"You don't have to say it," he said, coming back to her mouth. "I know all about you, Kathleen Somebody."

That brought her up short. "What do you mean, you know all about me?" She pressed her hands against his chest to push herself away so that she could look at him. "How do you know?"

He shrugged and smiled. "I know all I need to know. I mean, your name is Kathleen, which is a lovely name, and you're from the Avenue, and you work for Marie. . . . What better credentials can I get than that?''

For a moment a wave of pure relief swept over Kerry, and she relaxed slightly against his chest. Then sanity got the better of her and she pulled back again. ''But you're wrong,'' she said in a low voice.

''What?'' Tip seemed more anxious to get back to her lips than to get an explanation, for he only whispered his question while he made a swift foray in for a kiss.

''No. You're wrong, and I've got to clear the air. This has gone on long enough.''

Tip finally realized there was something wrong. He sat back. ''What's gone on long enough?'' he asked.

She looked at him for a long moment before replying. What on earth was she doing, sitting in her own apartment in the arms of a total stranger? Well, not a total stranger, but who he was made it almost worse than being in the arms of a total stranger. Yet Kerry was not sure why she had chosen this moment as the moment of truth. Was it because she wanted Tip to stop kissing her? Surely not. Kerry put it down to her basic honesty, tempered by a healthy dose of guilt, and pressed on.

''My name's not Kathleen. Well, it is, but I'm called Kerry. Kathleen Kerry Sullivan. Does the name ring a bell to you, Tip?''

At first he shook his head. Then he figured it out, and stared at her, comprehension and amazement widening his eyes. ''Sullivan. Kerry Sullivan. Of course.'' He let out a long, low whistle. ''You're Pop's partner. You're the other Sullivan.''

"Actually," she said softly, with much less acerbity than she should have, "it's you who's supposed to be the other Sullivan. I'm just marking your place til you come home; when and if you do, that is."

Tip just looked at her, his deep brown gaze probing hers until she felt the urge to look away. She hoped she hadn't sounded petulant or envious, but she wished she had sounded more pointed. Still, it didn't matter. Tip obviously got the point.

"I see," he said slowly. "This was supposed to be a stern lecture on filial responsibility, wasn't it? Did you and Marie set the whole thing up?"

"No, of course not! We had no idea we would see you tonight. How could we?" Kerry sat stiffly against the opposite arm of the love seat, twining her fingers together nervously. "I should have told you who I was as soon as we were introduced but I...something stopped me."

Somewhat to her surprise, Tip grinned. "I hope it was the same inclination that wound us up here." He indicated the couch with a wide stretch of his arm.

"I don't know what it was." She felt suddenly miserable and unable to come up with her well-planned lecture even now that the subject had been broached.

"I think I do," Tip said softly. "And I think I should have known, if I wasn't so wrapped up in impressing you back there in the Hampshire House." He chuckled. "I never met a hairdresser with your legal knowledge. Or your reading list."

In spite of herself, Kerry smiled. "It was a pretty dead giveaway, wasn't it?"

Tip nodded, then asked eagerly, "How's Pop been doing?"

Kerry flashed him a sharp look. "You should know the answer to that yourself," she said, with a trace of the sharpness she had been planning to summon.

"You're absolutely right. Old Tom and I...we tend to lose contact now and then."

"Tip. A year and a half is more than now and then."

He seemed genuinely surprised. "What makes you think it's been a year and a half? We had lunch together just a few months ago."

Now it was her turn to be surprised. "You did? He never told me."

Tip laughed. "I guess he wasn't aware he had to." He shrugged appealingly. "I know Pop tends to wax poetic on my behalf, but I think he and I have got a relationship that goes beyond my press clippings, dubious as those may be."

"But why...why haven't I ever met you before? I've been working for Tom for a long time, you know."

"I know. I hear all about you every time we meet. Pop sings your praises as highly as he sings mine, believe me. Although I must admit, if he had told me what you looked like, we would definitely have met sooner." He sighed and spread his hands out across his broad thighs. "There have been reasons for my staying away from the Avenue, Kerry. Pop understands them. He may not like them, but he does understand. And I hope you realize that I can't explain them to you right now."

Kerry was silent. It had never occurred to her that Tom might not be telling her everything he knew about his son. And, come to think of it, Tip could easily have visited before she came to work full time in the office the year before. They could certainly have visited at home, although Kerry could not imagine Tom entertaining in his rambling house off the Avenue. She had been there once or twice to pick something up for Tom and had been appalled at the total clutter that reigned. She wondered whether the house had been straightened up since Tom's wife had died five years previous. He hated anybody "messing with his things."

Tip leaned forward and took her hands in his. "So, Kathleen Kerry Sullivan, attorney-at-law. What's the verdict? Does this change anything between us, or can we pick up where we left off?"

Kerry looked at him. "I honestly don't know, Tip. All this happened so fast and so differently from the way I'd imagined it would."

Tip grinned. "You really were planning to read me the riot act, weren't you?"

Kerry had to grin back. "I was planning to prosecute to the full extent of the law."

"And now?"

"Now?" She pursed her lips and tried to think. "Now I don't know. I guess it's a lot for me to digest in one night. I feel torn...."

"Then I'll leave." Tip didn't sound in the least bit put out, but his voice was quite firm, and he stood up.

"You're really going to leave?" Faced with the reality of his proposition Kerry wasn't so sure it was what she wanted.

He nodded. "When it happens between us," he said gently, "I want it to be complete. No doubts. No indecisions."

Kerry felt her stomach drop at the sensual promise his words held. "What makes you so sure it is going to happen?'' she asked, her voice slightly hoarsened from wishing it would.

He held out his hand and pulled her to her feet. ''If there's one thing Pop bred into me, it's confidence, Ms. Sullivan. Now, kiss me good-night and give me something to dream about.''

Kerry pressed her body against his, fully expecting the kiss to evolve into a repeat of their earlier embrace. But, although he drank deeply and passionately at her lips and his hands moved across her back and up her ribcage in an expert sweep of arousal, he broke free after only a few moments. ''I'll see myself out,'' he whispered against her hair. At the door, he turned and winked. ''See you on the Avenue,'' he said and disappeared.

Chapter Three

Tip was true to his promise, although Kerry would not have called it a promise. Nor would she have been surprised if, after that one strange and lovely evening, she had never seen or heard from Tip again. The morning after, she had awakened feeling a mixture of chagrin and dismay. Chagrin because she had allowed herself to be seduced by the fragrant, warm night air and Tip's considerable charms, and dismay because she still wished that he had not left so abruptly.

But she managed to put him out of her mind by throwing herself into the Billy Stuart case with a fervor that was unusual even for Kerry. She spent the morning at the district courthouse, plowing through red tape until she was granted permission to read Mrs. Ranieri's statement about Billy Stuart. In the course of that day and the next she made three visits to Miss Carpenter's house and two to Mrs. Ranieri's. Miss Carpenter insisted that she would not lift a little pinky to help old Tom Sullivan until he apologized to her for his "awfulness," although she wouldn't tell Kerry what the awfulness was all about. Mrs. Ranieri, on her part, was considering increasing the charge to aggravated assault. She said she had a terrible bruise to show for it, but that she wasn't about to show it to anybody from Sullivan and Sullivan.

Kerry returned to her office that afternoon feeling slightly disgruntled again. Although she had rarely encountered any hostility on the Avenue, she felt that Mrs. Ranieri and Miss Carpenter, however hostile they might be toward each other, were united in looking upon Kerry as an outsider. Obviously the fact that she worked for Tom wasn't helping matters, but Tom, who seemed to be involved in something "big"— which meant a lot of his time was spent in the Gaelic Pub—refused to take either woman seriously and left it to Kerry to handle alone.

She was rather surprised to find Tom at the office, and actually had been hoping that he would be gone so that she could slip out and meet Marie at Carson Beach to cool off. But there he was, and she saw it as an excellent opportunity to finally pin him down about Miss Carpenter.

Unfortunately, she didn't realize until it was too late that Tom was not alone. She banged into the office, feeling hot and short-tempered. "Tom, I've had just about enough of Elsie Carpenter's silliness," she announced abruptly. "If you're not going to help me out on this, I don't know what I'm going to be able to do for Billy Stuart."

"Oh, for God's sake. Is old Elsie giving you trouble again?"

At first Kerry assumed it was Tom speaking, although he sat right in front of her at his desk and she hadn't seen his lips move. But it sounded enough like Tom so that she did a double take. Then she saw Tip emerging from the alcove where they kept a small desk and a telephone for "sensitive" conversations that could not be conducted in the open office.

"Elsie Carpenter is a jackass," he added amiably. "Always has been, always will be."

Kerry gaped. Tom said nothing, merely folded his arms across his considerable girth and grinned. Tip appeared to be appreciating Kerry's stare, for he grinned broadly. "Hi," he said needlessly.

"Kathleen Sullivan," said Tom, his voice oozing pride. "I'd like you to meet my son, Thomas Sullivan Jr. Better known as Tip. Tip, Kerry."

"Actually, Pop, we've already met," said Tip, but he extended his hand and picked up Kerry's, which she had been too surprised to offer. "It was purely by accident, of course, but we were introduced by a mutual friend just the other night." He squeezed her hand warmly while pumping it up and down.

"You have? Kerry, you never told me." Tom's voice was full of reproach.

"I . . . uh . . ."

"It must have slipped her mind," Tip offered gallantly, then added sotto voce, "Although I haven't been able to think of anything else."

Kerry opened her mouth to say something again and then shut it. She was too off balance to trust her voice yet and was glad that Tip still held on to her hand. Tom looked at the two of them standing before him and beamed.

"Well, sit down, sit down, both of you. Kerry, Tom's been telling me about his latest case. I think you'll find it interesting in the extreme."

"Oh, I think we should discuss Kerry's current crisis," insisted Tip. "What kind of trouble has the redoubtable Miss Carpenter gotten into this time?"

As soon as he released her hand Kerry sat down, not at her desk, but in one of the chairs reserved for clients. "I thought you weren't supposed to come to the Avenue," she said to Tip. Although she was glad that he had come to the Avenue, she was suddenly anxious on his behalf.

"Well, it's a slow afternoon," Tip said offhandedly. "I hadn't seen my pop in a while and I figured I could make a quiet appearance with nobody in particular the wiser."

"You know that's impossible on the Avenue," Kerry reminded him. "Tom always tells me the windows have ears and the walls have eyes."

"Tom's usually right," Tip conceded with a fond glance at his father. Then he turned back to Kerry and smiled his private smile. "In this case, however, I felt it was worth the risk."

"Okay, Kerry." Tom apparently felt that the introductions were over. "Now that we have the most brilliant legal mind in the business at our disposal, let's go over the Stuart case." He settled back farther in his chair to listen, and Tip, tossing his oxblood leather loafers carelessly across his father's desk, did the same thing.

Kerry had no choice but to go into a brief description of the case and where she stood at the moment. As she spoke she was aware of an increasing embarrassment. The petty details of her little job seemed to grow with each word she uttered. What a waste of a good lawyer's time, she found herself thinking! To have to deal with a bitter and prejudiced old woman, an angry old maid and a half-wit. She knew she was being uncharitable, but she couldn't help hearing her story through Tip's ears and imagining how tacky and two-bit it must all sound to him.

Tip, however, appeared to have no such reaction. He listened carefully, even asking a question every once in a while to clarify a point. When Kerry was finally finished, he turned to his father. "Sounds like we could make a nice countersuit against Louise if we can get Elsie to testify, don't you think, Pop?"

Tom squirmed uncomfortably in his chair. "Yeah, but you know what that means, son." He rolled his eyes and reddened.

"Yup. And so do you. And I think it's time you got over your silly pride and did something about it, too." He spoke sternly, and Tom's discomfort deepened.

"What on earth is this all about, Tom?" Kerry demanded. "What could you possibly have done that was so terrible?"

Tip laughed. "You're not going to believe it, Kerry. Tell her, Pop."

Tom hemmed and hawed and finally came out with the tale. It seemed he had been inundated with complaints several years before, when Elsie Carpenter had owned a houseful of cats. Her neighbors, and Mrs. Ranieri was chief among them, had insisted on bringing charges against her on the grounds that the feline community was a health and safety hazard. Not only had Tom done the deed, but he had also, quite inadvertently and with no malice, run over one of the cats late one night as he was pulling away from the Gaelic Pub. Elsie, it seemed, was prepared to forget the lawsuit, which, thanks to Tom's expertise, was settled out of court, but she could not forgive the death of her kitty.

Kerry listened with amusement; it was just the sort of talk one heard on the Avenue, and the kind of thing that, strangely enough, endeared it to her. "Well, Tom," she said when he had finished. "I think Tip's right. It's time you took your hat in your hands and apologized. Do it for Billy Stuart."

"Hummph. Yes, well, maybe you're right. I'll...take the matter under advisement." Tom placed his finger alongside his nose and paused. "So tell us, Tip, my boy," he began brightly, anxious to change the subject, "what's this big case you've been working on for so long? I know Kerry's dying to hear all about it."

"He's right," Kerry admitted. She looked at the old Seth Thomas clock on the wall. Four o'clock. She was supposed to meet Marie at four but decided that Marie would have to wait. This was more important than a swim in the semipolluted waters of Carson Beach.

"Well, there's really not much I'm at liberty to discuss right now," Tip began. "All I can say is that it involves a big ring of criminal activities that covers just about most of the eastern part of the state and just about every crime you can think of. Illegal gambling, laundered prostitution money, loan sharking—you name it these guys are doing it. And they're doing it on a big scale. They've got a well-established hierarchy that spreads itself nice and thin, so nobody knows who's running the show. Of course, that's our job, to find out who's running the show. And it hasn't been easy, believe me. This is definitely the toughest case I've worked on so far."

"Well, Tommy, you'll crack it sooner or later. Any progress with the Mafia connection?"

Tip shook his head. "Nothing. I think it's a dead end. These guys are independents, although I still can't figure out where they're getting their operational funds." He turned to Kerry. "The big problem is we're coming up with a lot of little busts, petty stuff that doesn't amount to a hill of beans in the overall picture. But a lot of little people are getting victimized; people in this neighborhood, as well as downtown and on the North Shore. What we need is one important collar, linking one good bust to a chain of events, and then I think we'll hear some nice singing."

"Did you investigate that other connection you were mentioning?" Tom asked.

"Yes. We've got some good stuff on the guy, but . . ." Tip pulled his chair closer to Tom while Tom bent forward across his desk. Father and son embarked on a long, low-voiced conversation, the details of which escaped Kerry, who wasn't sure if she was supposed to be listening or not. She sat in her chair, trying to look interested but not nosy, wondering what they were talking about with their mention of shunt operations, back-tracks and double exposures.

It was not legalese that she could decipher, but she suspected that it came from the Sullivans' long exposure to street talk and street behavior. That was what made them both such good lawyers—they had witnessed life from both sides of the street. Kerry had to admit that in that sense, as well as in their clearly greater wealth of professional experience, they left her far behind. She thought again about the Stuart case and frowned, despite a feeling of having betrayed poor Billy Stuart in her heart.

Still, she couldn't help feeling left out on a personal as well as on a professional level. She had thought at first that Tip's unusual visit to the Avenue had been on her behalf. And she had been flattered, although she had made an attempt to play it cool because she didn't want Tom to know the extent to which she and his son had become intimate in such a short time. But now, as father and son put their heads together, giving every evidence of having forgotten she existed, Kerry began to wonder. Had Tip really wanted to see her again or had her reminder the other night merely prompted an overdue visit? She remembered the confidence with which he had told her that he wanted her to be completely sure of what she wanted before they got together. Had that been sincere or simply a clever way of sliding out of an awkward situation? Kerry did not want Tom to know about Tip's visit to her house. Did Tip feel the same way? Had he changed his mind about her when he found out who she was?

Clearly she was not going to get any answers to her questions here and now, Kerry thought. She might as well go to the beach and get some sun before it got too late. She rose, making sure that her chair scraped loudly against the worn wooden floor. Maybe the fact that she was leaving would induce Tip to remember why he had come.

But Tip and his father beat her to the punch. Just as she was about to announce her departure, they rose as well, obviously not having heard her preliminary commotion. "I think he'll be there right now," Tom was saying. "He usually spends his afternoons there and his mornings too, far as I can tell."

"It would be great if we could get him to talk," Tip said, straightening the collar of his already impossibly neat pin-striped shirt. He was clearly getting himself into a business mode. "I sure could use some leads on that Greg Harvey fellow, and at this point I'll take whatever I can get."

"Oh, he'll talk," said Tom. "A few beers under his belt and he'll spin us a fine yarn, you can be sure."

"Yeah, but how much fact will be in it?"

"Ah, Tommy, that's for you to decipher." Tom looked concerned for a moment. "I just hope there's no one in there today that you don't want to see, know what I mean?"

Tip spread his fingers, palms up at shoulder height, and flashed his most charming smile. "What? A guy can't go tip a few with his old man on a Saturday afternoon?" He laid a hand on Tom's shoulder. "Don't worry, Pop. I can handle whatever comes up."

Tip turned around and, on doing so, nearly tripped over Kerry, who was standing exactly where she had risen, trying to figure out what to do with her arrested departure scene. "Kerry!" Tip looked surprised, as if he had literally forgotten her presence. "Are you coming with us over to the Gaelic?"

Of course she would have loved to have gone. She was dying to find out more about Tip's mysterious case and to see who it was he wanted to talk to, and who he wanted to avoid. But she didn't like the way her invitation came as an afterthought, however sincere it had sounded. And she knew, without looking at Tom, that he felt her presence would cramp the Sullivan style. She felt a defensive flare of anger and shook her head.

"No thanks. I've got plans to meet someone at the beach and I'm late already." As proof, she held up the striped canvas beach bag that had been dangling indecisively at her side.

"Oh. I see." She didn't know whether he disbelieved her or was waiting to hear who it was she was planning to meet, but in either case she was in no mood to tell him now. She tried to ignore the disappointed look on his face as she went to the door. Tip, she knew, could be a very convincing actor when he chose to be. It was part of his golden boy charm.

"Well," she said, still reluctant to leave on several counts. "I guess I'll be seeing you around the Avenue." She tried for the same jaunty tone he had used with her when he left her apartment, but didn't think it sounded convincing.

"I guess so." Then, just as she was about to close the door behind her, Tip said. "Hey!" Kerry stopped, her heart jumping. She turned around and faced Tip's smile. "Maybe I'll see you around the Common, too. That violinist is pretty terrific, and I find myself there quite a lot lately."

Kerry opened her mouth to say she'd be delighted to meet him there, but he raised his hand and waved and then turned back to Tom. Once again she was left with her mouth hanging open and nothing to say. She stomped out of the office, thoroughly exasperated with all the Sullivans, including herself.

Kerry would never have gone to the Common that night if she hadn't been subjected to a thorough brainwashing by Marie at Carson Beach. She had expected Marie to be full of sympathy at the inexplicable perfidy of the male race, but Marie had surprised her and had left Kerry feeling that nobody she knew was behaving as she expected them to these past few hot summer days.

"Well, tell me all about it!" Marie had said excitedly as soon as Kerry spread her towel beside her. "Was he terrific last night?"

"Nothing happened," Kerry said glumly. "He kissed me and went home."

"Oh, honey," Marie commiserated. "I think you need a few lessons from Aunt Marie on how to prevent such tragedies."

"It wasn't such a tragedy. I don't know why I ever let myself get talked into it anyway. He's certainly not worth the effort."

"Are you nuts?" Marie looked as if she truly believed this. "Tip Sullivan not worth the effort?" She patted Kerry's hand. "Believe me, I happen to know you're wrong. Woman's intuition, and in my case it never fails. I know he's good."

Kerry rolled her eyes to the blazing sun. "Marie. One of the few points on which we disagree is the importance of sex in our lives. And I don't happen to think tip Sullivan is worth the effort, for any reason. Besides," she added honestly, "I doubt if he considers me worth the effort either."

"Ah. Now we're getting somewhere. What happened?"

So Kerry told Marie about that afternoon's office visit and its outcome. "He doesn't exactly sound as if he was obsessed with seeing me, wouldn't you agree?"

Marie made an exasperated sound. "Kerry Sullivan, you are the stubbornest person I've ever met. What d'you want, an engraved invitation to the next Kennedy bash?"

"Perish the thought!"

"Well, it sounds to me like he'd like to see you again, but he's just not sure about you. After all, you were the one who hemmed and hawed your way out of bed with him the other night. What's he's supposed to do?"

"If he had really wanted to see me—" Kerry began, but Marie hooted her down.

"Listen to you! And you're supposed to be a liberated woman. What's the matter, you can't make any moves yourself? Honey, if old Marie waited for the men to do the job she'd be a very lonely lady. Now you listen to me, Kerry Sullivan. If you're even remotely interested in this guy, you damn well better make an effort. He said he might be on the Common, so just show up there tonight! What harm can it do? If he's there, you'll have a blast, and if not—" she shrugged "—you'll get to hear some nice music. But if you want to see Tip Sullivan, get off your butt and do something about it!"

"I'm not even sure I do," muttered Kerry, who at that moment truly was not.

"Ufff! I give up! Come soak your head in the water. Maybe that'll knock some sense into you!"

So they had swum and sunbathed and had not discussed Tip Sullivan again. But later that evening, sitting in her apartment with a book unread on her lap, Kerry found she was straining to see if she could catch the sounds of a violin. After an hour of this frustrating nonactivity, she finally conceded that Marie was right.

"You are being ridiculous," she told herself as she went to find something to change into. Despite her budgetary restrictions and a basic conservatism when it came to clothes, Kerry's one vice was an addiction to Filene's basement, the world-famous bastion of bargains, where she was able to stock up on her favorite style of casual sportswear even on her salary. She tried on three combinations, decided one was too formal, another too casual, and finally, pulling on her original white jeans and striped V-neck T-shirt, left the apartment before she could change again.

It was not as hot as it had been the past few nights, and Kerry could feel a sweet breeze ruffling the hairs on the back of her neck. She was glad she had come out of the house, even if her mission did not prove successful. And, walking alone, she had to remind herself that there was a very good chance it would not. After all, Tip had only casually mentioned the Commons as a meeting place, perhaps only to make things easier for himself. It was entirely possible that he wouldn't even show up on the Avenue for another year or so, and he wouldn't have wanted to commit himself to anything definite with Kerry in Tom's presence. Besides, she reasoned as she headed down the Hill, the Commons was an extremely unlikely place for Tip to hang out. A chance meeting was one thing, but for him to habituate a place like that was hardly likely.

And anyway, Kerry reminded herself, she still hadn't made up her mind about Tip Sullivan. She had a lot of old, unfavorable baggage floating around inside her head on his account, and his behavior on the Avenue earlier had not entirely dispelled it. Yes, he had behaved responsibly toward his father, which answered her initial complaint about him, but he had behaved pretty cavalierly toward her, and she wasn't about to let that go unnoticed just because he was playing the dutiful-son role so well.

By the time she reached the stand of birches and the rotunda she had pretty much convinced herself, not only that Tip would not be there, but that she didn't care if he wasn't. It was a lovely night for a stroll, and already the sounds of sweet violin music perfumed the air. Even the local drunks seemed to be making themselves scarce, and Kerry settled against a narrow young birch trunk to listen to the violinist weave his magic tunes.

Of course, she was looking for Tip as well, although she forced her gaze to roam casually around the area and did not allow herself the eager search she would have liked to have made. Her initial inspection proved that he was nowhere to be seen. There were very few people, as a matter of fact, and those that were not strolling casually by were definitely in pairs. There were stars out, but no moon, so if anybody stood beyond the small circle of light thrust by the single spotlight, that person would be in almost total darkness. Kerry trained her eyes on the musician, refusing to be caught peering into the darkness.

It was because she was staring directly at him that Kerry was the first to see what actually happened. Well, not what happened, but certainly its effect. Still, even though she was staring right at it, she couldn't believe what she saw.

At first she thought it was part of the musician's act. Just as he swept his bow through a high crescendo of illuminating sixteenth notes that seemed to fill the air and then hang there like an afterimage of light, he dipped suddenly forward and fell to his knees. It looked natural enough, as if the violinist had been carried away by his own music. Kerry even had an impulse to raise her hands and applaud.

Then she saw a dark stain on the man's white shirt. At the same time, she realized that she had heard an additional sound along with the cascade of notes. And she knew what it had been, even though she had never heard it before. It had been a pistol shot. And the bullet had struck the violinist in his left shoulder, just beneath the violin.

Although it seemed to Kerry that she was paralyzed for an eternity with the horror of what had just happened, she was actually the first one to reach the stricken musician. Her feet carried her across the grass and up the three stone steps without her realizing what she was doing, and she knelt to catch the man just as he slumped from his knees to the ground. She caught his head in time to keep it from striking the marble floor and even managed to pull the violin from his grasp before it was crushed beneath his body.

Kerry wasn't really in control of her responses—she was too shocked. She was vaguely surprised at how light the man felt in her arms, his torso spread across her knees and his head resting in her lap. His face was quite pale, but his eyelids fluttered, and his mouth moved as if he were trying to say something. She bent closer but could not hear a word.

A quick check of the wound revealed that it was high on his shoulder and therefore, she hoped, not fatal. At first, there didn't seem to be much blood. There was so little, in fact, that for a single confused moment Kerry thought she might have been mistaken. She shifted around to look out at the crowd, and then she saw Tip.

He was moving through the trees swiftly, shouting something indecipherable to someone she could not see. Behind him ran a stocky man holding something long and straight in his right hand. At first Kerry thought it was the flutist from the other night. Then she realized it must be a man with a gun.

It was impossible for Kerry to assimilate the scene. Tip, running through the trees, apparently chasing a gunman or else being chased by one. Her mind went blank at the possibilities, and she looked down again at the victim. Suddenly she was aware that there was blood, a lot of it, and it was flowing all over her white pants. How will I ever get this out? she thought irrelevantly, and then came to her senses and shouted for someone to call an ambulance.

"One's on the way!" someone shouted, and Kerry, looking up again, thought she saw Tip, staring at her in midflight. But it had not been Tip's voice she heard, and the darkness was now a chaotic flutter of people running in every direction. The entire scene took on the grim, floating sensation of a nightmare and Kerry was not even certain she had seen him that first time.

She become totally involved with the victim, who began to writhe and moan, making the blood flow even faster. Kerry found a cloth, apparently something the musician had used for his violin, and tried to staunch the flow while she calmed the man down. She didn't know how long she sat there with him, holding his head and whispering soothing nonsense while her own terror mounted by the moment. Finally, a trio of white-coated men came running up with a stretcher, accompanied by two policemen and several men in suits.

"Who is he? Who are you? What happened? Why are you here?" They all asked questions at once, hovering like flies over a pat of butter. Kerry felt panic constricting her throat, and she had to resist the urge to scream at the top of her lungs just to clear the air.

Finally one of the men escorted her away and the medics surrounded the victim with their efficient storm of activity. Kerry let herself be led away by one of the policemen to answer questions down at the local precinct. Despite the warmth of the night, she found she was shivering uncontrollably and could scarcely speak through chattering lips.

There was only one thing of which she was glad during the rest of that nightmare night. Somehow, despite her shock and disorientation, she had managed to do something very canny. At the moment before the authorities arrived, instinctively and having no idea why she was doing it, Kerry had slipped one of her business cards from her pocketbook into the musician's pants pocket.

"Call me," she had whispered urgently into his unresponsive ear. "Call me if you need help."

Chapter Four

Kerry barely remembered being driven to the police station that night. The blaze of flashing lights that surrounded her departure and that of the ambulance from the Boston Common was fused in her mind forever afterward with the fear and confusion that paralyzed her mind. She had a vague recollection of a knot of people parting as she was led through the trees to the waiting squad car, of hushed voices that could not conceal their urgent curiosity.

It was eerie to be led along by the stocky plainclothesman, knowing that most of the bystanders were wondering if she were criminal or victim. With his hand firmly attached to Kerry's upper arm, the man executed several sudden turns to avoid the crowd, so that she was yanked unceremoniously back and forth, and felt like both criminal and victim. She was also getting dangerously dizzy and spent most of her energy convincing herself not to cry or faint.

Once at the station, a big, grim building that loomed over the twisting narrowness of New Sudbury Street, things seemed to calm down and clear up. She was taken into a quiet room, where a police matron handed her a large cup of strong, steaming coffee and sat with her, mercifully silent, while Kerry recovered both her wits and her composure.

"I'm a lawyer, you know," was the first thing she said.

The matron, although clearly not impressed by this information, nodded politely and accepted the card Kerry pulled from her small purse. She remembered, for the first time, having made the same gesture to the wounded man, and she shuddered.

"You need another cup of coffee?" asked the matron.

"No, thanks, I'm fine, now."

"'Kathleen K. Sullivan; Sullivan and Sullivan,'" read the matron. She looked up quizzically. "You a partner? Already? You look kind of young."

Kerry smiled. She had heard that before. "It's a small firm," she replied.

The matron apparently was not particularly curious. "Well," she said, rising, "If you're okay, I'll go tell Stan. He's the one who'll be questioning you."

"Stan?"

"Stan Wykoff. He's chief detective in charge of homicide." And, without another word of explanation, the matron left, leaving Kerry with a sudden sharp void in the pit of her stomach. Homicide? Then that meant the man had died. The wave of dizziness she had felt earlier returned, and she laid her head on her arms for a minute while this awful news sank in. Despite all her experience on the Avenue, she had never taken any part in a murder trial, much less been witness to one herself. She felt vulnerable and alone.

"Hey? You okay?"

Kerry looked up to see a man standing in front of her. He looked so much like a caricature of a homicide detective—short, stocky and rumpled, with a cigarette hanging out of one corner of his mouth—that Kerry had to resist the urge to smile in disbelief. His appearance was strongly reassuring.

"Everybody seems to be asking me that," she informed him in a strong voice. "How okay am I supposed to be after seeing a man get killed, having him die in my arms?"

"Die? Who said anything about dead?" Detective Wykoff sat, or rather sprawled, in the chair across the table from Kerry's.

"The matron said you were the homicide detective."

Wykoff grinned lopsidedly. "Yeah, but she didn't say it was a homicide, did she? There's a difference between homicide and attempted homicide, you know. As a lawyer, you should certainly know."

"How did you know I was a lawyer?" she asked. In answer, he merely flicked out the card she had given the matron. "Elementary," he said dryly, and she had to grin.

"So, you're with old Tom Sullivan, up there on the Avenue, eh? I know old Tom. How come I never met his pretty partner?"

Kerry decided to let this bit of chauvinism pass unremarked. "Fortunately, we don't get many homicides, attempted or otherwise, on the Avenue these days."

"That's because old Tom keeps a close eye on his people," Wykoff remarked. Then, before Kerry could say that she doubted Tom's influence went quite that far, he added, "I know his son, too. Tom Jr. You know Tip?"

At the mention of Tip's name, Kerry got a sudden, vivid flash of the man, half in shadow, who had been running through the trees. Once again, she was sure she had seen Tip at the gazebo. She must have paled, because the detective leaned forward, suddenly alert. "Anything wrong, Miss Sullivan?"

Kerry opened her mouth and then shut it. Instinct and legal know-how told her not to say anything until she was absolutely sure of what she had seen. "No, nothing's wrong." She smiled at Wykoff. "How do you know Tip?"

"Oh, we've worked together on this and that. He's an up-and-comer, you know."

Kerry shrugged off this familiar accolade. "I hardly know him. Now, Detective, I think I'm ready to begin."

"Okay, let's have it. Everything you remember, however insignificant it may seem. You know the procedure, I'm sure."

He was right; she did know the procedure. Slowly, and with deliberate care, Kerry recounted for Detective Wykoff and the note-taking uniformed officer who had slipped into the room, exactly what she remembered in the order that she remembered it. She told of her urge to get out of her hot apartment, of her recollection of the skill of the violinist in the gazebo, of standing in the clearing facing him and how she had been staring directly at him when he fell to his knees. She mentioned that she had heard the shot after he fell, but Detective Wykoff said that witnesses often registered the audio portion of a traumatic event after they have seen it happen.

She told them that she had run forward even before she had realized what had happened, and recalled the way the dark stain had grown on the violinist's white shirt. She described in exhaustive detail what she thought she had seen going on around her while she attended to the fallen musician.

Wykoff commented that people are often more aware of their peripheral vision than they think they are.

Kerry told him that she had been aware of a lot of motion, but that she hadn't seen anything recognizable, and that she wasn't even certain from which direction the shot had come.

"Are you sure, Miss Sullivan?" Wykoff asked, leaning forward and hitching the collar of his rumpled sports jacket over his shoulders. "Are you sure there wasn't anything, or anyone you could describe to us? Anything at all that was even noteworthy or mentionable?"

Kerry had to use her best courtroom demeanor to escape those probing eyes. "No," she said firmly and patiently. "I'm quite sure I've told you everything I remember, Detective." Even as she lied, Kerry was asking herself why she had bothered. Was it because she really had been mistaken and the vision of Tip had been merely a figment of her imagination, the result of wishful thinking? Or was she unconsciously moving to protect him and, if so, from what? She had no idea what he had been doing in the dark. *Had* he been chasing someone? Or was it Tip who was being chased through those birch trees?

"Why, then, did you put your business card in the victim's pocket?" Wykoff asked suddenly, flashing her white card out of his shirt pocket like a magician. There was not the slightest hint of smugness in his voice, but Kerry winced. She should have known they would find it.

She shrugged, trying to make light of it. "Just force of habit, I guess. People in trouble often don't know where to turn, and it sometimes helps to have a place to start." She paused and smiled. "I know it may sound like ambulance chasing to you, but believe me, this is the first time I've ever found a potential client who was actually in need of an ambulance."

Wykoff stared at her expressionlessly, without blinking, and Kerry managed to keep her face calm and utterly unrevealing. It was a trick Tom had taught her. All she did was think about taking her law boards and concentrate on that awful blankness that had overcome her when she'd been trying to dig deep into her brain for an answer. The ruse seemed to fool Wykoff.

"Well, Miss Sullivan," he said at last. "I want to thank you for your help. I wish all my witnesses were as careful and painstaking as you've been."

"I've been on the other side of that table," she told him. "I know how important full disclosure can be." Even as she said it, Kerry was remonstrating with herself. Liar! How can you say that with a straight face? Aloud, she said, "I would appreciate a little information from you, though, Detective Wykoff. Can you tell me a little bit about what's going on here, and why homicide is handling the case even though the victim was not killed?"

Wykoff sent a silent message to the note-taker, who quickly left the room. When they were alone, he lit another cigarette before talking. "Under normal conditions, Miss Sullivan, I wouldn't be at liberty to tell you anything. I'm still not—not technically, at least. But I'm gonna use my instincts and fill you in, since you seem to be a pretty smart lady, and you'll probably put it together soon enough for yourself. Cigarette?" Kerry declined and waited impatiently as he puffed in silence for a moment. She was finally beginning to feel the edges of fatigue and the windowless room full of smoke was not helping a bit.

"Well, as far as we can tell, this was just an isolated shooting. Somebody with a grudge against this violinist—his name is Claudio Partero, by the way— just came up and blew off a shot and then disappeared into the night. It happens all the time, you know."

"Not as often as that," Kerry said evenly. "And the police usually have some idea about why it happened, especially if they're putting homicide on the case."

Wykoff grinned. "Tom Sullivan's got a hot one with you, don't he now? But you happen to be wrong. We're usually sadly in the dark about motive. It's generally the last thing we can figure out."

"There were an awful lot of policemen on the scene very quickly," Kerry pointed out. She hadn't really thought about it until that moment, but she knew that she was right. Aside from the two men who had first questioned her, there had been at least half a dozen others fanning out under the trees, and at least that many squad cars had been parked on Tremont Street where she had been taken to the car. "You don't get a dozen men on a call within two minutes of an isolated shooting. And you don't get homicide people right away."

"Sometimes you do," Wykoff said, but he saw that Kerry wasn't buying it, and he stubbed out his cigarette with a grimace. "Okay, Kathleen. I can see you're not gonna let me off the hook. Jeez, you lawyers!" He lit yet another cigarette before going on. "I can't tell you much, but I can tell you that we've been...involved in that area of the Common, I mean surveillance ya' know, for a while now. There's been...we think somebody might be using that little gazebo area as a meeting place, or a drop for some kind of illegal activity." He stopped when he saw her raise her eyebrows in question. "Sorry, kid, I can't tell you anything beyond that. But that's the reason we were so well covered. That's why there were so many cops."

Kerry was silent for a minute, trying to extract the nuggets of real information from the detective's words. She knew quite well that there was more to the story than he was telling her. "And you don't think there was any connection between the violinist's—between Mr. Partero's—shooting and the activity you've been monitoring, is that right?"

Detective Wykoff looked genuinely surprised. "No, of course not. The guy was only an itinerant musician. He may have fooled around with somebody's girlfriend or been late on a loan for his fiddle there, but he's not involved in any crime ring.'' He smiled winningly. "That would be pushing coincidence too far, don't you think?"

Kerry didn't bother saying what she thought. Fatigue was beginning to blur her vision as well as her mind, and suddenly all she wanted was to go to sleep and forget about everything for a while.

Wykoff noticed her weariness and jumped to his feet with surprising alacrity. "But you don't want to talk about this anymore, do you? You must be very, very tired. God knows you've had a tough day, and I don't suspect old Tom lets you off lightly at the office, either. Let me get a car to take you home, Miss Sullivan. You've been a tremendous help, and I doubt we'll have to bother you again with this nasty business.'' He helped Kerry to her feet and put a paternal arm around her as they moved toward the door. "Of course, should we need to get in touch with you again for any reason . . ."

"I know, I know. Don't leave town, right?"

He laughed delightedly. "Right! Don't leave town. But really, try to put it out of your mind. We don't want you having nightmares, do we? You got a friend who can come stay with you tonight? Female or otherwise?"

Kerry straightened up and his arm dropped off her shoulder. "Listen. I'll be just fine. Thanks for your concern. Goodbye."

"Goodbye," he replied, obviously not aware that he had offended her. "Oh, and by the way, Miss Sullivan?"

Kerry turned to see him smile and flick her business card with his nicotine-stained thumb. "I'll see that this goes back where it came from, all right?"

She nodded curtly but did not reply. She could feel his sharp eyes following her all the way down the hall. That guy didn't tell me everything he knows, she thought to herself. Of course, she hadn't been totally honest with him, either. All in all, she would have to call the encounter a draw.

As a uniformed policeman drove Kerry to her apartment, the darkness was beginning to wane. The fatigue she had been fighting all night began to get the upper hand as they drove through the deserted streets. Also, being out of the insulated safety of the police interrogation room and on the wide open streets reminded Kerry of the brutality she had witnessed just hours ago. She felt fragile and fragmented, and she looked at the few loiterers who wandered on the Hill with new fear.

The squad car turned up Chestnut Street slowly, and Kerry found herself hoping that the noise of the tires on the cobblestones wouldn't awaken her landlady, who slept on the first floor and would surely give Kerry notice if she saw her being delivered to her door at four A.M. by a police cruiser. But she could not see any motion behind the stiff lace curtains in the semi-darkness and decided that even nosy Mrs. Anderson wouldn't be awake at this hour.

"You want me to see you in?" asked the young cop when they pulled to a stop in front of her building.

Kerry smiled weakly. She was regretting that she hadn't called a friend from the police station. All her bravado had disappeared during the short ride home. But she shook her head. "No, thanks, I'll be fine. I just need to get some sleep."

The patrolman nodded. "You do that. Take a sleeping pill or something and just forget this whole night."

"I wish I could, officer," she said fervently. "I really wish I could."

But, although she smiled and waved as he pulled away down the narrow street, she knew that forgetting would be impossible. Even sleep would elude her, she was sure, until she had sat down and made some sense out of the bedlam that had intruded on her life.

She stood out on the silent street for a moment and reminded herself that this was her neighborhood and that there was no reason to be afraid of it all of a sudden. The breeze was sweet with a slightly salty tang from the east, and the red brick that curved up on all sides of her was beginning to pale with the coming dawn. Kerry couldn't shake the feeling of being exposed and vulnerable, and she turned quickly to her doorway, holding her key out in front of her like a weapon.

Just as she spun around, she caught sight of someone out of the corner of her eye. In a second her heart had speeded up with a hammerlike urgency, and she heard herself gasp loudly as she swung out with her extended arm. The figure dodged and cursed and then revealed itself in the light of the doorway.

"Tip! You idiot! You nearly... why did you... oh, Tip!" And then Kerry surprised herself and Tip by bursting into tears.

"Hey! I'm sorry, I didn't mean to scare you. I was just..." He saw her face and caught her chin in his palm. "Hey! Are you...are you all right?"

"Of course I'm not!" Kerry wailed. "I'm miserable and I'm scared, and you frightened me half to death! I wish everybody would stop asking me if I was all right!"

"Okay, Okay, it's all right now, I'm here...I'm here." He gathered her against his chest and let her stay there sobbing until his cotton shirt was soaked through. One hand absently stroked her hair while the other held her tightly around the shoulders so that no more fear could get inside the little circle of warmth he created.

Finally it was Kerry who had to say, "We could get arrested, standing out here like this. I don't want to go back to that awful police station for a long time. Come on in."

She gave him the key and allowed him to guide her up her own stairs, through her own door, and onto her own couch. She was numb with shock, fear and fatigue, and her only thought was that she was glad that someone, anyone, had come to rescue her from her own panic.

Tip disappeared and Kerry could hear him rummaging around in her tiny kitchen. He returned with a glass of milk and a bottle of Courvoisier, dusty with disuse.

"Where'd you find that?" she asked, surprised.

"In the cabinet over your fridge," he told her. "There's a card still attached to it. 'To Kerry,'" he read, "'but only if you'll share it with me. Love, Phillip.' Who's Phillip?"

Kerry wrinkled her brow. "I haven't the faintest idea," she confessed.

Tip laughed and sat down beside her on the couch. "Then this must be very old cognac indeed." He opened the bottle and poured a liberal amount into her milk glass.

"Milk and cognac? Yech!" She made a face.

"Warm milk and cognac," he corrected, holding it to her lips. "Very good for what ails you, no matter what ails you. Tom taught it to me. Drink."

"Tom would never dilute his spirits. Not in a million years," Kerry observed but took a dutiful sip nonetheless and found it surprisingly good.

"You're right," Tip said, clasping his hands behind his head and stretching his long legs out in front of him. "But he swears by it for everyone else in the world."

Kerry took another, longer drink, and then surveyed him over the top of the glass. "What are you doing here, anyway, Tip?"

"Oh, I don't know. I thought you might need some company after what happened."

"How did you know that I might need some company?"

Tip straightened up and leaned forward. "Hey, if you don't, I'll be glad to leave you alone."

Kerry's hand shot out and grabbed his arm, forcing him back against the couch. He grinned, but she did not return the favor. "I said, how did you know I might need some company? How did you know what happened?"

He stopped smiling. "I have friends down at headquarters. Stan Wykoff called me. Said he had a little lady lawyer who asked a lot of questions." He reached up and swept a strand of hair out of her eyes. "Aren't you glad he didn't call Pop first?"

Kerry ignored this. She was trying to decide whether to ask Tip if he had been at the gazebo earlier that night. Now would be the time, she told herself. Ask him now and get it out in the open. It's no use going on wondering whether you saw him or not. Just go ahead and ask! But the way he was looking into her eyes, half smiling and half yearning, made it very difficult to say anything at all.

Kerry got up suddenly, sloshing some of her spiked milk on the rug. She felt she had to move around, or she would be sucked into a languorous slumber—a soft, yielding place that left no room for questions about shootings, for the hard, cold facts of life. She moved deliberately away from the couch, as if to look at Tip would be to invite that languor to steal over her.

"I have to figure it out," she muttered, mostly to herself. "I just have to think about it, and then I can..."

"Think about what?" Tip was bent over, mopping up the spill with his own handkerchief.

"About what happened tonight. I have to get it all straight in my mind before...I just can't relax until I've figured it out." She began pacing the room a bit unsteadily, trying to force her mind to focus on the events of the evening.

"Didn't you tell everything to Wykoff? Didn't you get it straightened out there?"

"What did Wykoff tell you about the whole thing?" Kerry asked suddenly. "What do you know about all this, anyway?"

She couldn't keep the accusing note out of her voice. Tip raised his palms defensively and shook his head. "He only told me what he thought I needed to know, Kerry," he said gently. "Now, why don't you come back and sit down and tell me all about it. Maybe talking it through one more time without a cop breathing down your back will help."

It was impossible to avoid the candid charm of that voice, the clear and generous offer of help. Kerry moved back to the sofa without a bit of reluctance, cursing herself for being so paranoid. It was just the night, she reminded herself. The night, and the cognac and everything.

She sat down, took one more small sip, and a deep breath. "I just didn't feel like staying inside last night," she began, omitting any mention of the fact that she had hoped to meet Tip at the Common. "You know, it was a nice night, and I felt kind of restless, and...and I remembered how beautiful that violinist—his name is Claudio Partero—sounded. I just...I just wanted to get out of the house for a while. So I walked down there, and sure enough, he was playing, and..."

As she spoke, going through the now familiar litany of events, Kerry felt herself relaxing. She leaned her head back against the edge of the couch, staring up at the ceiling as she talked. Her own words were acting like a soporific, as much as the cognac and Tip's soothing presence. She did not notice Tip moving closer, leaning forward so that he could stare at her face, drink in the soft plane of her cheek, gently lit by a golden-shaded table lamp. The amber light tipped her short hair with fire, and he could see the shadow of her eyelashes elongated across her upper lids, extending the line of her almond-shaped eyes.

She didn't notice him until, looking down to take a sip of her drink, she found his face directly in front of hers. Normally she would have been surprised and, given her current state of exhaustion, probably would have exclaimed aloud and perhaps even have spilled her drink over both of them.

But strangely enough, she wasn't at all surprised to find his deep brown eyes sparkling quite close to hers or his mouth slightly open in a smile that did not indicate amusement but something altogether different. She merely blinked once and allowed him to remove the drink she still held in her hand and to set it carefully on the desk nearby.

"Don't mind me," he said in a soft, syrupy voice. "Just keep on talking."

Kerry opened her mouth, then shut it and shook her head. "I don't think . . ."

His voice got even deeper and thicker. "You don't think what?"

"I don't think I want to talk anymore right now."

His face moved an inch closer to hers, so that she could feel his warm breath on her face and see the flecks of black around the irises of his eyes.

"You know what?" he whispered.

"What?" Kerry could feel her body melting into an agreeable state of liquid as he pressed closer against her.

"I think you've probably done enough talking for the evening. I don't think talking is what you want to be doing at this point."

Kerry slid a little farther back against the cushions, both to accomodate Tip's body and to allow the pleasant sensations that were rising from her loins to have free rein. "I agree. I don't think that's what I want at all."

His lips grazed hers, seemingly only in passing, but the touch was electric, erotic beyond belief. Kerry closed her eyes and opened them slowly, savoring the sensation and the anticipation.

"What do you think you'd rather be doing?" Tip inquired, making a brief, butterfly-light pass at her throat, lingering a bit longer than before. He shifted his body so that this thighs pressed against hers and his chest brushed against her breasts and ribs. Kerry lifted one arm and traced a line down the side of his face, not quite touching his smooth, tanned cheek.

"It's hard to tell," she said, staring at the imaginary line she had just traced.

"I understand." Tip caught at her hand and kissed the tips of her fingers. "It's really late, and you must be just exhausted."

"Somehow," she murmured, leaning back so that he could take advantage of her invitation to kiss her throat again, "somehow I don't think I could go to sleep just yet."

"I understand," he said again, obliging her with a trail of feathery, fiery touches all the way down to the beginning of her breastbone, where it disappeared into her T-shirt. "All the excitement, the trauma. Clearly, you need to relax."

He looked up, his eyes full of heat and humor. She met his gaze, smiled and shook her head. "No. That's not what I need at all. I need you to kiss me, Tip Sullivan. Right now."

And suddenly she meant it urgently. He complied, gathering her up with a force that belied the lazy foreplay in which they had just indulged. He groaned and pulled her over onto his lap, pressing his mouth to hers with such need that it knocked the breath out of her.

Kerry was more than willing to return the gesture. Whatever doubts she had had about Tip Sullivan regarding either his feelings for his father or his activities earlier that night, she now found it easy to put them out of her mind. Ever since she had first laid eyes on the man, this was what she had wanted to do with him.

Everything else that had happened in the past two days was erased from Kerry's mind with an ease that she might have found shocking if she hadn't been in the grip of such a powerful sensual attraction. She forgot about the Common and the gazebo, forgot even about that awful moment that she had been so sure would be emblazoned on her mind's eye forever. All she could think about or see or feel was the pleasure of Tip's embrace, and her only thought was to get closer, to have more of him.

But Tip was taking it slowly, measuring his arousal in carefully calibrated doses and moving with a slow, cool deliberation that contrasted excitingly with the passion of his touch. Kerry soon found herself falling in with his leisurely yet ardent pace, exploring every inch of his fragrant skin like the treasure it seemed to be.

Kisses came first, around the face, with particular concentration on the lips and behind the ears. His touch was alternately urgent and languid, so that just when Kerry felt she could not breathe under the assault of his hungry mouth and tongue anymore, he would pull back and rain soft delight around the perimeter of her lips, moving up and down her heart-shaped chin and into the soft declivity of baby-smooth skin between her neck and her ear. Every once in a while they would stop, look at one another and smile before resuming their luxurious assault. Theirs was a mutual effort with a mutual attraction behind it, and for once the two lawyers found themselves without need of speech. Their mouths would have been far too busy to bother even if they had been able to think of something to say.

But speech would have been extraneous. Their bodies were perfectly articulate, perfectly in tune. They spoke the same language, right down to the smallest nuance of gesture and intention. When Tip moved his lips down across her collarbone and between her breasts, Kerry knew that she was meant to explore the region just beneath the collar of his shirt, delving her fingers into the strong musculature of his shoulders and up the firm bulge of his arm through the sleeves. Then a slight inclination of his head, and she knew it was time to sit forward while he lifted her T-shirt over her head and slipped her bra straps down and off so that she was naked from the waist up. She waited a moment or two, exquisitely aware of her own breasts, small but full and aroused to hard tips by the heat from his gaze. Then she leaned forward and unbuttoned his pin-striped shirt, starting at the bottom and working up until she could slip it off his broad shoulders and leave him in the same state as she.

Only then did they allow themselves to press together to experience that first shocking pleasure of bare flesh on flesh. Tip's hands ran up and down the smooth, narrow expanse of her back while her fingers stroked the strong line of his spine, playing along the fretwork of muscle and tissue that fanned out from it. She could feel the accelerated thud of his heart against her own ribs intertwined with her pulse in an inextricable rhythm.

Then Tip lifted himself away and bent his head to her nipples, and Kerry lost herself in the fireworks of her own arousal. She could no longer pretend to any deliberation but wrapped her arms and legs around him in a frenzy of passion. But Tip would not abandon the pleasure of licking and teasing her breasts into quivering anticipation and dipping occasionally into the even more tender flesh on the sides of her breasts. It wasn't until Kerry heard herself moaning slightly with urgency that he stood up and pulled her up beside him and worked first on her pants and then his own until they both stood nude in the pale, cool light of dawn.

Tip led her back into her own bedroom as if she were a stranger in her home and he the host. He walked backwards so that he could stare at the nip and flare of her tiny waist and slightly full hips, never seeming to miss a step or to falter. For her part, she was entranced by the broad smoothness of his torso, hairless and bronze except where his loins sprang up, erect with wanting her, out of his coarse and curly mat of hair.

They fell in a tangled heap on top of her old satin counterpane, not bothering to sort out their arms and legs as they clasped together and moved into the rocking cadence of their lovemaking. His body on top of hers threw a deep shadow over Kerry, blocking out the growing light so that all she could see was his chest heaving and his face looking down into hers with acute desire. He kept his eyes open and riveted on hers so that, as much as she wanted to close her eyes and abandon herself to the growing ecstasy, she could not. His gaze commanded her attention, demanded her total commitment to the motion that was carrying them both up a roller-coaster peak of climax.

It happened simultaneously for them, and Tip threw his head back just at the moment when Kerry knew she could not spend one more mote of energy in gazing at his face. She closed her eyes and called out in a soft little moan and slipped with him down the long, swift nether side of pleasure, losing sight of everything but her own ecstasy, for what seemed like a very long while.

They remained entwined even after their hearts had stopped racing and their breathing had slowed to a normal pace. Still deep inside her, Tip rolled over so that they lay side by side, their bodies making contact at every possible point, and their eyes searching each other's faces for affirmation of what they both knew had just transpired.

"I'm trying to think of something witty to say," he murmured against her ear at last. "But for the first time in recent memory, I appear to be at a loss for words."

"Lawyers are all alike," Kerry said. "We don't think we can finish with anything unless we've given the final argument."

"We do spend an awful lot of time using our brains and our mouths," Tip replied. "It's nice to be so eloquent with our bodies for a change."

Kerry just nodded and then turned to look out her window, where the pink of dawn had already given way to the silver of daylight in the eastern sky. "I can't believe this night is over. I thought it would go on forever, earlier." She turned to him and smiled, suddenly shy. "Then I wanted it to go on forever."

He kissed the tip of her nose. "The only thing I can't figure out," he murmured between kisses, "is how on earth this didn't happen sooner. I mean, it feels like it was supposed to have happened a long time ago." He took a deep, shuddering breath and his eyes smoldered with remembered passion. "All that pleasure, just waiting to escape. Why didn't I meet you before, Kathleen Kerry Sullivan?"

Kerry chuckled. "Maybe Tom was afraid neither of us would get on with our work if we met. Maybe he knew this might happen."

Tip laughed and nodded. "I wouldn't put anything past my pop, that's for sure." He lifted his fingers and traced languid circles across Kerry's taut belly. "But I have a feeling Pop would approve if he knew."

She reached down to stay his hand. "Oh, you won't tell him, though, will you?"

Tip's eyes widened in surprise. "Why not? Why shouldn't I?"

Kerry shrugged uneasily. "I don't know. I just feel . . . don't tell him, okay, Tip? I just think it would be more . . ." She wasn't sure how to finish the sentence, but a deep streak of conservatism seemed to have surfaced at this unlikely moment, and she was certain that she did not want Tom to know she had been to bed with his son. It wasn't merely because Tip was virtually a stranger and she didn't want Tom to think her "loose"; she was certain, deep down, that she and Tip were already intimate on more than the physical level. It was more that Tip was Tom's son, and that might complicate things at the office, for her or for Tom or for Tom in his relationship with Tip. Either way, she was quite sure she didn't want it to happen—not yet, anyway.

"You just don't think it would be right and proper, is that it?" Tip finished for her, smiling gently. "Okay, Kathleen. I think it's the Kathleen in you talking now. I won't mention a word to the old man, not yet, at least."

Kerry kissed his palm, grateful that he had echoed her last thought, as well as for the fact that he had agreed.

"But don't expect me to be able to keep my hands off you for long in the office. And if you think old Tom won't be able to figure things out from the way I look at you, then you've underestimated the old man."

"You're right. I just feel..." she let her voice trail off softly. Sleepiness was stealing over her again.

"Hey." Tip bussed her nose again. "You never did get to get that off your chest, about what happened last night. You still feel like telling old Tip?"

"Nope." She shook her head. "Somehow it all seems very far away right now, which is just where I want it to be." And it was true. The specter of the violence to which she had been witness was only a shadow of a memory behind the curtain of satisfaction and fatigue.

"I guess you'd like to get some sleep now, wouldn't you?" Tip inquired softly, moving his arm to cradle her head behind her neck.

"That might be nice," she whispered lazily.

Tip resumed the lazy circling of his fingers on her breast and belly, moving down between her legs, where he stirred her weary body anew. "On the other hand . . ." he said, his lips against hers.

"On the other hand . . ."

"I move for a retrial. What do you say, counselor?"

Kerry shifted to allow him access to her waiting body. "I have no objections. No objections at all."

Chapter Five

Kerry finally drifted off to sleep around six, planning to catch only a short nap before getting up and going in to the office. But the next time she opened her eyes, the sun was high in the sky and someone had turned on her window fan to move the air about as the heat of day soaked through the brick walls.

At first she didn't remember anything, but lay beneath the sheet reveling in the most delicious lassitude, wondering why her whole body felt so loose and at peace. Usually she woke up quickly and hopped out of bed to begin her day without a second thought. This morning she stretched each limb with tender solicitude, unwilling to relinquish the pleasant lethargy that covered her body like a cool breeze.

Then, in quick succession, she remembered: Tip, their ardent lovemaking earlier that morning, and the reason for his presence in the first place. She sat bolt upright in the empty double bed, her eyes wide, her hands suddenly damp with sweat.

"Hey!" She looked around, unsure if what she remembered was real or a terrible and wonderful dream.

"Hey yourself!" The voice from the living room reassured her. "I'll be there in a second. Lie back down. Don't move until I get in there."

It was an order she was glad to obey. Now she could hear Tip's muffled voice issuing from the other room. From the sound of it, he was talking on the phone. "Yes, I know," he was saying quietly. "You think we can do an *ID* based on that . . . ? I haven't been able to find that out yet. . . . No, I don't know. I don't think so, but I don't know." There was another pause. Then, his voice slightly louder, he said, "Corrigan, I said I'd do what I can. Now just take it easy, will you? Everything's under control. I don't think we've got anything to worry about from that end. Just relax, will you? I'll be in touch."

He hung up and soon appeared in the narrow doorway to her bedroom, holding a tray carefully with both hands. "Good morning, sunshine!" he said merrily. Kerry sat up, smiling. "Oh, no, don't sit up! Don't sit up." He waved her back down with his chin. "I'm having enough trouble balancing this damned thing as it is without the sight of your luscious upper torso to distract me." He pretended to avert his eyes until he reached the side of the bed and placed the tray gingerly on the bedside table. Kerry, meanwhile, pulled the sheet discreetly up to her shoulders.

"It looks like your bedside manner could use a little practice." She grinned up at him.

"I'm a lawyer, not a doctor, remember?" He leaned over and pushed her back down against the pillow. "But I don't remember you complaining last night, counselor."

Kerry lifted her arms around his neck and kissed him. "Nothing to complain about. I feel lovely this morning in spite of the fact that I should feel terrible. What time is it?"

"Nearly eleven."

"Eleven?" She sat up quickly again, nearly knocking Tip's teeth out. "God, I've got to hustle. I've got a case working, and Tom'll be frantic if I don't show up!"

"Relax!" He pushed her back down again, rubbing his lip. "I've already talked to Tom. He was frantic, especially when those idiots from Division B called him at eight this morning looking for you. But I've filled him in a little, and he said to take your time. You don't have to come in at all today if you're not up to it."

"Ohhhhh." That meant that Tom knew about her and Tip. But Tip apparently had read her mind.

"As a matter of fact," he added conversationally, "I called Tom, so he had no idea where I was calling from. He was just relieved to hear that you were all right."

Kerry raised her eyebrows apologetically. "Sorry. Listen, Tip, I don't want you to think I'm...I'm ashamed of this or anything." She took his hand and caressed it gently, lowering her eyes so he would not see her chagrin. "It's just that..."

"Forget it," he replied briskly. "I understand completely. You're probably right. Now come on, sit up and eat your breakfast. It's not every day that I serve one of my masterpieces to a member of the public at large." His eyes glittered as Kerry sat up, revealing a stretch of brown skin and soft curves. "No matter how intimately I've been acquainted with the at-large."

"Tip." It was half remonstrance, half entreaty. Kerry wouldn't have minded another lovemaking session in bed, especially seeing Tip sitting there, looking so crisp and clean and handsome. The contrast between his preppy image and the unbridled lover of a few hours before was undeniably arousing.

Shaking his head, Tip answered, "Uh-uh. It's business time, lady lawyer, much as I'd like to think otherwise. Now eat, and then we talk."

For the first time Kerry inspected the contents of the little antique Coca-Cola tray which he had brought her, thoughtfully covered with a linen napkin from her meager collection.

"You certainly made yourself at home in my kitchen," she mused out loud, noting that he had found, in addition to the linen, her china sugar-and-cream set as well as a tiny bud vase, which he had filled with a spray of dried baby's breath from a larger bunch on her desk.

"I think I've earned the right," he said, smiling intimately.

"But what on earth is this?" she asked, surveying the pale pile of indecipherable food that lay on her plate.

"That's my masterpiece," he replied in a slightly injured tone.

She looked up and smiled weakly. Eating first thing in the morning was not her forté. "What's in it?" she inquired, trying to sound interested.

"It's just grilled ham and swiss cheese, open faced on a slice of whole wheat toast. I usually use Gruyère, but you were out of Gruyère."

Kerry, who had tasted Gruyère only once in her life and hadn't liked it much then, did not argue this small point. The sandwich sounded innocent enough. She lifted it gingerly to her mouth.

"Sorry about the way it looks," Tip observed, watching her take a bite. "I'm not used to using that Teflon you have, and it got kind of sloshed around in the pan."

"It's very good!" Kerry observed. "There's a taste in it I can't quite figure out. What's under the ham?" She chewed ruminatively, trying to decipher the pleasant undertaste.

"Oh, that? I just spread the bread with a couple of slices of mashed banana."

"Mashed . . . !" Kerry nearly choked.

"Of course. It adds that little touch of sweetness, not to mention a whole lot of potassium. You need potassium, you know. Lucky thing you had a ripe banana on hand. It doesn't taste as good when the banana's not ripe."

Kerry smiled, gingerly put down the sandwich and lifted her teacup to her mouth. Tip laughed at her expression. "Okay, so it's an acquired taste. Now finish your tea, at least, and get dressed, so we can talk without you driving me crazy. I've got a few more phone calls to make."

He left her to abandon her breakfast and find something to wear. She pulled out a sundress in a bright floral print with a row of ruffles down the back, then decided it looked too childish and rejected it in favor of a sleeveless cotton blouse and matching skirt in a pale toast-and-white stripe. By the time she came out Tip had ensconced himself in her desk chair and was holding the phone to his ear while he jotted something on a notepad. "All right. Yes, I've got that. Thank you." He hung up and smiled as he saw her approach. "You look fresh and lovely and utterly irresistible."

She sat down on the couch and returned the smile. "You look pretty amazing yourself, considering that you're in yesterday's clothes. How do you do that?"

"It's an old trick I learned. When you go to Harvard on a Dorchester Avenue budget, you have to learn how to preserve your wardrobe." He walked over and sat down next to her but not close enough to allow any contact. "Now. I think it's time we did a little talking about what happened last night, don't you?" His eyes searched hers and he grinned again. "Not after you came home," he said softly. "Before."

Kerry nodded. She had been putting it off long enough. She knew the horror she had witnessed was not going to go away just because she had other much more pleasant things to think about.

As she had done at the police station with Detective Wykoff, she began at the very beginning and told him everything she could remember, right down to the description of a dress she had been admiring on a passerby. When she got to the part where Claudio

Partero had been shot, she paled and he put a comforting hand on her shoulder.

"I know how hard it is to keep going over and over these things, Kerry. It seems like you'll never be able to get them out of your brain if you keep on having to repeat your story again and again."

"I know, I know," she agreed sadly. "I've told that to witnesses myself a hundred times. I guess I just never realized how hard it can be, both to talk about it and to forget it."

"Well, if you've told that to witnesses then you also know that sometimes talking is the only way to forget; the only way to exorcise that demon of memory." His voice was gentle and reassuring, and Kerry realized what a very good lawyer he must be with his persuasive skills.

"You're right." Taking a deep breath, she went on with her story; how she had run forward without thinking and thus had been the first to arrive at the scene, how she had caught Claudio Partero in her arms as he fell, and how the weight, the dead weight of his body, had caused her to fall to her knees. She shuddered at the memory, which was still imprinted so strongly on her body as well as her mind.

"And then?" he asked. "Then tell me exactly what happened. What did you hear? What did you see? What did you think you heard or saw?"

Kerry looked at him sharply. "You sound like you have more than a passing interest in this case, Tip. Why all the questions?"

He returned her gaze for a moment before replying. "Would you believe just a lawyer's professional curiosity?"

She shook her head slowly. "Not for a minute," she told him.

He sighed. "I didn't think you would." Then his eyes narrowed. "But why not? You saw something, didn't you, Kerry. You're not certain you saw it, but you think you did, and you didn't tell Wykoff about it. Why not?"

For a long time there was complete silence in the room. From her bedroom, Kerry could hear the whirring of the fan that was sending little gusts of cool air into the living room. She could hear the garbage trucks down on the street, and the noise of children as they passed by her building four floors below. Her wall clock seemed to tick with maddening lethargy.

"I saw you," she said finally, not taking her eyes from his face. "At least, I was pretty sure I saw you. But afterwards, I wasn't so sure. I mean . . ." She lowered her eyes for a moment. "I had been hoping to see you, you know, so I thought it might be possible that it was just a figment of my imagination, that it was just . . . that I just made a mistake. That's why I didn't bother to tell Wykoff. I didn't think it could have been you."

He shook his head, smiling sadly. "Why not?" he whispered. "Don't you think I was hoping to see you, too?"

She took a deep breath. "I didn't know," she replied simply.

He nodded. "I understand. I felt the same way. But that's not what's important right now. Tell me what you saw, what you thought you saw me doing."

"What I thought . . . what I'm pretty sure I saw," she said carefully, "was you, running behind a stand of trees, right after I heard the shot. I couldn't tell if you were chasing someone, or if you were being chased. I remember thinking, why on earth would Tip be chasing someone? Or why would he be being chased? At first I didn't connect it at all with what had just happened, everything was moving way too fast for me to make any sense out of it. And later on...well, later on I just figured that I had to have been mistaken. That it couldn't have been you." She raised her eyes to him. "But it was you, wasn't it, Tip. You were there, and you were running, weren't you?"

Tip stood up and went to the bay window and stared out over the rooftops with his hands thrust in his pockets. He looks a little like his father, Kerry thought, standing there rocking back and forth like that. A little, but more like himself, like what she wanted him to look like: tall, strong, and handsome. She tried to repress a wave of desire for him.

He sighed audibly and turned around. "You're right, of course. It was me, and I was running. I was running in the hopes of finding the guy who fired the shot, and the guy you saw behind me was Detective Woods, of District B, who happened to be working the area undercover at the time. We didn't find anybody, of course. The area from which the shot was fired emptied out like a punctured balloon. Not a soul around, and no witnesses either, of course." He pounded his fist into his palm. "Damn! I wish it hadn't been you! I wish it wasn't you that got messed up in this thing!"

All at once he sounded like the Avenue, like his roots. She looked up at him, surprised by his vehemence. "Messed up in what thing? What was happening down there last night, Tip? Why was there an undercover cop and why were you there? Why did Claudio Partero get shot?''

The demand in her voice could not be ignored. He came back to the couch and sat down wearily. "I don't know why he got shot, Kerry. I wish to God I did. And I can't tell you much about what was going on near the gazebo last night, but I'll tell you as much as I'm allowed." He took a deep breath. "For the past three months my office has been investigating a group of men who have been engaged in all sorts of illegal activities. I hesitate to call them a gang, because they're much too sophisticated for that. Call it an organized ring of victimizers. They do a little bit of everything—extortion, pimping, drugs, smuggling—but their main things are gambling, payoffs, loan sharking and all the attendant crud that that involves.'' Tip's distaste was evident in his expression. "Anyway, we know they've got several haunts throughout the city, places where they meet to exchange money, to make plans and, occasionally, to exact payment of one sort or another. The gazebo is one of those spots, and the A.G.'s office, in cooperation with the police department, has had it staked out for a while now. That's why there was all that heat as soon as the shot was fired. At first we all thought that it was related to our investigation.''

"And now you don't, is that it?''

"Right. Now, given the fact that this guy Partero has no record and no connection whatever with this whole business, there's no reason to suspect that our gang had anything to do with it. I think it was just an isolated case, a coincidence.''

"That's what Wykoff said," Kerry said thoughtfully. "But are you sure of that? Couldn't that bullet have been meant for someone else, and hit Partero accidentally?"

Tip pursed is lips. "It's nominally possible, but I doubt it. First of all, we didn't see any of the regulars around last night, either to shoot or to get shot. And secondly, Kerry, when those guys shoot, they don't usually miss. Believe me. They never miss."

His expression was even more chilling than his words, but Kerry was not convinced. Still, she saw no point in arguing it, since Tip obviously had a lot more information at his disposal than she did. But she had to admit that she felt better, having had one mystery cleared up. She was glad that Tip had been there, for more than one reason. It meant that he had expected to see her. It also meant that she had not been hallucinating his presence.

He seemed to know what she was thinking. "Next time I want a date with you," he said with a smile, "I promise I'll make it at some more mutually agreeable spot. Someplace where the threat of violence is a little less marked."

She smiled back. "Yeah. A nice quiet walk through the Combat Zone would be a relaxing change of pace." The Combat Zone was a neighborhood notorious for it's strip joints and hookers, and they both laughed.

Then Tip gathered her in his arms. "I have to go now," he said against her ear. "I want to stay in the worst way, but I really have to go. Will you promise me that I can see you again soon? Like the next available minute you've got free?"

She nuzzled against his shoulder and nodded. "It's a promise."

He tipped her head back and kissed her long and tenderly, clinging to her lips as if he couldn't bear to be separated from her. Then, shaking his head in exasperation, he rose. "If I don't get up now I'll never leave you," he said hoarsely. "And the A.G. doesn't give time off for bad behavior." He smiled his brilliant smile. "See you soon, Counselor Sullivan. As soon as possible."

"As soon as possible, Counselor Sullivan," she replied, wishing that he didn't have to go.

"Oh, by the way, I almost forgot to tell you. You got a phone call earlier. Someone from the Boston City Hospital. They asked for Kathleen Sullivan, said they had gotten your card?" He looked puzzled. "Wouldn't leave a name, though. You know what it's about?"

Kerry shook her head. "Probably one of my clients from the Avenue. You know the way your father hands out those business cards. I've got clients I don't even know about."

He grinned and nodded. "I know the feeling. Okay, I'm leaving now." He made a face. "I must be nuts, but I'm leaving. Right now." He slammed the door deliberately.

Kerry waited until she could no longer hear his footsteps on the stairs before rushing to the phone. She hadn't wanted Tip to know, but something told her who it was that had made that call from BCH. And, if her instincts were right, she was just about to find out some very interesting information—from Claudio Partero himself.

It took her almost two hours to find Mr. Partero at BCH. Apparently fearing for his safety, he had registered under an assumed name, and Kerry had several long arguments with the hospital admitting desk trying to convince them that a man with a shoulder wound from a bullet had indeed been admitted the night before. Finally she found a sympathetic admittance nurse who was willing to confide that a "Mr. Viola" had been admitted with such an injury and that he might be found somewhere on the third floor, Ward D.

That turned out to be the easy part. The nurses who staffed Ward D seemed to look upon their patients as their private domain and did not take kindly to Kerry's prolonged prowling in the halls. One irate woman in white was about to call the hospital guard when Kerry wasn't able to come up with a room number on request. Fortunately a smallish man with a goatee overheard their altercation and stepped in on Kerry's behalf.

"Yes, yes, this woman is here for us," he said, taking Kerry's arm and nodding rapidly as he pulled her away from the surprised nurse. "Mrs. Sullivan, I'm so glad you could make it, but how could you have been so foolish as to forget our room number?"

"You never gave me your room number," Kerry hissed while maintaining a pleasant smile so that the suspicious nurse would not realize that she had no idea who the man was.

"Oh, yes, yes, so sorry, but when someone else answered your phone this morning we could not take the chance that it was a person we did not want to find us." The man looked quickly to his right and left as they turned the corner in the hall.

Kerry didn't know whether to be amused or worried by his obvious cloak-and-dagger act. "Who are you, anyway?" she asked, careful to keep her voice as low as his.

He flashed her a quick, white smile. "I am Emilio Partero, your friend's brother. But he is known here as Mr. Viola, so you may call me that as well."

"Okay, Mr. Viola." She did not bother to mention that the name was fairly obvious to anyone who cared enough to think about it and that others could easily be more successful than she had been at penetrating the security system the Parteros had set up. "But why all the secrecy, anyway?"

He raised and lowered his eyebrows meaningfully. "You will see, Mrs. Sullivan, you will see. Right in here, please." He ducked into a corner room, yanking her in after him.

Kerry's first thought was that there were so many people in the small room that she couldn't see the hospital bed. She counted only six people, but there seemed to be more because of the way they closed ranks when she appeared. They were all men, except for a tiny woman dressed all in black who sat in the one available chair.

"She's here," Emilio announced unnecessarily. "Mrs. Sullivan has come."

"It's Ms. Sullivan," Kerry amended, but nobody seemed to listen. They were all staring at her, apparently trying to decide if she passed some private test of theirs. She had no doubt that they were all members of the Partero family, either brothers or cousins, but clearly related. At last, on some unseen signal, the men parted and Kerry saw the bed. The man who lay in it was very slight and very still. For one heart-chilling moment she thought he might be dead. Then he smiled and she remembered that thin, dark face from the night before.

"Please come in, Miss Sullivan," he said, extending the arm that was not bound in bandages. Kerry moved through the crowd, which now dispersed on either side of her. A chair was produced, although Kerry noticed that the older woman had not been removed from the chair, where she sat industriously knitting and seemingly not aware of what was happening in the room around her. Kerry sat down and smiled at the man in bed. "Mr. Viola, I presume?"

His grin was delightful and infectious. "You'll have to excuse my family," he told her without any sign of embarrassment. "Most of them have only recently come to this country and they still hold some rather old-fashioned views of justice and injustice. This elaborate security network was Emilio's idea."

Kerry turned and nodded to Emilio, who bowed with courtly grace. "The head nurse on this ward would have been perfectly adequate," she murmured to Claudio.

He chuckled. "I suppose so. But my family thinks I have lost my senses and have become too trusting after being so long in this country. I was the first one to come here, five years ago, you see. They think that any man who is still playing music on the street after five years in the magic U.S. of A. has to have lost hold of something upstairs." He tapped his forehead.

"But you play so beautifully. It would be a shame if we lost the privilege of hearing you play."

"Thank you. I was trained at the conservatory in Milan, you know. My mother thinks the Boston Symphony Orchestra should have come begging for my services long ago."

"Your mother is right."

Claudio paused to translate this to his mother, who, although Kerry hadn't expected her to respond, nodded and murmured something in Italian.

"My mother says you are a smart woman—for a woman." He grinned, then grew serious. "She also wants to thank you for coming to my aid last night. You may have saved my life."

"I don't think—" she began, but he cut her off.

"And I want to thank you, too. You may have been more help to me than you know."

She looked at him, puzzled. "Perhaps you should begin at the beginning and tell me what happened last night from your point of view."

Claudio shrugged, then winced and placed his hand gingerly over his wounded shoulder.

"Oh, I forgot to ask. Is everything all right? With your shoulder, I mean?"

"Unfortunately, it may not be all right," Claudio told her sadly. "The doctor thinks there may have been some nerve damage. The bullet sheared off quite a lot of muscle, and bone tissue as well. It looks like there will have to be a few operations, at the very least." He made a rueful face, which did not disguise his pain. "I may not play again for a very long time."

Kerry was silent for a moment, for she recognized the blow this was to a man whose whole life was his music. "Now tell, me," she said urgently, "how did this happen to you?"

"I have been playing at the gazebo there for a long time, now," he began. "I started playing there as soon as the weather got warm enough for my violin, and I was there last fall as well. I know what goes on in that little clearing as well as what goes on in my own home."

Kerry thought of Tip and his investigation. "And what goes on there?" she asked softly.

Claudio frowned. "It's hard to put into words, Miss Sullivan. You see things night after night and they begin to take on a pattern, but it may not be as easy as that to describe to someone who has not seen it." He took a deep breath. "There are men," he went on, "men who come to that spot on a regular basis. They are not the kind of men you would want for your friends, Miss Sullivan, believe me."

"What do they do there, Claudio?"

"I couldn't say for sure, but I'm fairly certain they exchange quite a lot of money. There have been times when bags, paper bags, and suitcases have been passed back and forth, but I couldn't say what was in them."

He paused, clearly remembering something else. "What else, Claudio?" Kerry prodded. Her lawyer's instinct was roused, and she was beginning to get excited.

Claudio sighed. "You know, a street musician sees a lot of things, Miss Sullivan. Sometimes a lot more than he wants to see. But it's usually best to pretend that one doesn't see them, and to concentrate on the music instead of the audience. That way, one can never be sure, and one can always comfort oneself with the thought that it probably wasn't what it seemed to be."

"Claudio, what else do you think you saw?" Kerry asked, remembering how reluctant she had been to answer the same question from Tip. "I know it's hard to commit yourself to something like this but I can assure you that even without my being your legal counsel, this information will be privileged—between you and me."

"I saw guns, Miss Sullivan," he said at last. "On many occasions, I have seen guns. But I've never seen one used until last night, when it was used on me."

Kerry knew she was holding her breath. "Claudio, this is very important. Now, are you saying that you believe that shot was intended for you?"

He nodded. "I think it was."

"Why?"

"I told you why. I have been playing in that gazebo for a long, long time. Those men, the ones who...conduct their business there, they would have to be very stupid not to figure out soon enough that I have seen a lot in my nights there. That man—the man who shot at me—obviously figured it out, and he is sure to tell the others about me sooner or later—if he hasn't already." He paled and a shudder ran through his thin frame. "So you see, once they know they would be fools not to realize that I am in the way, shall we say? Even if I do not understand all that is going on."

"And do you, Claudio?"

"Do I what?"

"Do you understand what's going on? Could you identify the man who shot you last night?"

The room was utterly silent, and Kerry could feel the entire Partero family waiting for his reply. "I could," he said softly. "I probably could. And I think I have a pretty good idea of what he and his friends are doing."

Kerry's heart fell at the word "probably," but she did not have a chance to say anything. Suddenly all the men were talking at once, mostly in Italian. It wasn't until the mother raised her voice briefly that the hubbub died down and Emilio stepped forward.

"Mrs. Sullivan, this is why we brought you here today. Claudio told us of your help for him last night and of the way you offered help to him in the future. You are a lawyer, a good lawyer, and we want you to help us find justice for our brother. We want someone to pay for what has happened, for his ruined life."

The speech was dramatic and effective. Even the mother stopped knitting and nodded gravely. Only Claudio remained unconvinced. "This whole thing was their idea," he apologized. "They think that if you can catch the man who did this to me and prosecute him, perhaps I can get recompense."

Kerry thought quickly. "You know, Mr. Partero, I can't prosecute anyone on your behalf, if that's what you're interested in. So far it's the state's case and you're just a witness—if, that is, they can make an arrest at all. But your family might be right," she went on. "You might be able to get restitution in a civil suit, although I'm not sure. But the main thing is we have to get the state to bring criminal charges against the man first. All I can do there is act as your advisor, since witnesses have no need for legal representation. Once we get that, we could press for civil damages.

That way, even if you don't get recompense . . . well, there's something to be said for revenge, isn't there?''

He looked at her for a while before replying. "Yes, it would be nice if it were possible.''

"It might be possible, Claudio.'' In her mind Kerry was already arranging the legal arguments she would make, the indictments she would ask for, the charges she would press in civil court once the criminal case had been established by the state. She was so often on the defense that the very idea of being involved in a prosecution, even a civil prosecution, made her mouth water.

"Possible, yes,'' Claudio replied. "but not very smart, don't you think?''

"Why not?''

"Miss Sullivan. The people who did this to me . . . I don't know much about them except what I see in the gazebo every night. Really, there is not much I could say about them that would hold up in a court of law. Even I know that much.''

"You're not trying to bust the entire crime ring, Claudio. We're only trying to bring one man to justice for what he did to you.''

"Ah, but that's the problem. That one man is one of many. And, even though I might not know much about them, I'm afraid of what they think I might know. They already suspect me of suspecting them. If I were to come forward, what do you think they would imagine?''

Kerry had no immediate answer to this question. She knew that Claudio was right. But she also knew that he had a legitimate case on his hands, and that if he didn't come forward with an accusation, the police would just assume that it was an isolated incident or, at the worst, a private family matter. So far the state didn't have much of a case, and not much in the way of suspects even if they did. Either way, in the absence of witnesses, suspects or a victim willing to talk, they would have very little reason to continue the case once they found—*if* they found—the man who fired the shot. And she happened to know that they had other, bigger matters on their minds.

But *she* didn't. What did she have besides the Billy Stuart case, which promised to be long, boring, and probably fruitless? A case like Claudio's, which aroused all of her legal and social antennae, didn't come along every day. She ached to sink her teeth into it. But as yet, she had not been formally asked.

It was a delicate situation. First the state's criminal case would have to be established. Then, in order to institute civil prosecution, the victim would have to agree to have her prosecute on his behalf. The family was obviously eager to proceed, but Kerry knew that without Claudio's cooperation she would have no case at all. At best it was going to be tricky. She would need Tom's legal mastery to drive this thing through the courts. At worst, she would end up a fool, and Claudio would end up—no, she couldn't let herself think about that. Such things simply didn't happen in this day and age. There were such things as police protection, as a competent judicial system which would make it difficult, if not impossible, for street justice to be exacted in the way Claudio imagined it might. And, she reasoned further, she doubted that any sophisticated crime ring would bother to rush to the rescue of a man accused of a personal crime like assault with a dangerous weapon. They would not think a civil case worth their time and effort. If she handled it right, the whole question of what Claudio knew or did not know would never come up.

No, the worst thing would be if the case never got to court at all. *That* would make Claudio a sitting duck.

Kerry smoothed down the material of her skirt before she spoke. "Claudio, I would be willing to take on this case for you. That is, my partner, Mr. Tom Sullivan, and I would be glad to take it on together. We will act as your advisors in the criminal proceedings and then handle the civil suit. But we must have your full cooperation, and for that, you must be fully convinced that it is in your best interest for us to procede."

"Do you believe it is, Miss Sullivan?"

She nodded gravely. "Yes, I believe it is. I think you will be safer in the long run if you step forward and bring the man to court—for shooting you, and not for anything else."

"I see." Clearly, he was not convinced. Kerry knew what to do. Rising, she smiled at the silent assemblage.

"I think it would be best if I gave you some time to think about this, Claudio. For the time being I won't mention this to anyone, and neither, of course, should you." Kerry thought about Detective Wykoff and repressed a guilty sigh. "Talk it over with your family, but you must remember to do only what you feel comfortable about doing. This is your issue, and yours alone."

She tried to look sternly at the others to remind them not to interfere unduly, but she was met with opaque stares from seven pairs of eyes. It wasn't until she got to the door that Claudio spoke again.

"Miss Sullivan?"

"Yes?" She turned, her heart in her throat.

He smiled weakly. "Would it help if I told you the man's name?"

She swallowed before answering so that her voice would not come out in a squeak. "Yes. I think that would be a big help."

"His name," said Claudio in a slightly stronger voice, "is Greg Harvey. And I think he meets with his friends somewhere else, too. I once heard them mention the beach house at Carson Beach."

She nodded, managing just barely to keep her excitement under control. Greg Harvey—she had heard that name before. And she knew the abandoned beach house he was referring to. "Thanks, Claudio. That'll help. Now you relax and I'll get things started." She smiled. "And tell your family they can go home and get some rest. Everything's going to be all right."

He smiled, but he didn't look as if he believed her.

Back at the office Kerry had an even harder time convincing Tom.

"Kerry, you can't get involved in this! You were a witness. You know you can't get involved."

"Tom, I wasn't a witness because I didn't see anything. I was just the first person to reach the scene of the crime, that's all. There's no law that says a lawyer can't get there first, is there?"

"If there was," Tom retorted glumly, "half the ambulance chasers in this town would be out of work."

"Well I'm not an ambulance chaser. But I do know a good case when I see it. That man's livelihood has been destroyed by a bullet, and he believes he can identify the man who fired it. If the state prosecutes this Harvey guy, Partero could be an extremely damaging witness—with our help, to see that he doesn't get himself into trouble. He's not only got a good criminal case, but I think he might have a pretty sound civil suit, too."

"Boy, you are thinking big these days, aren't you?" Tom seemed unusually glum, and Kerry wasn't sure why. Either he had been more worried about her than she'd thought, or he was irritated at having to spend the entire day in the office alone and miss his lengthy afternoon "meeting" at the Gaelic Pub. Probably a little of both, she decided fondly. "What about Billy Stuart?" he inquired testily. "Are you going to forget all about him?"

Kerry grinned. "I wish I could, but you know I won't. Unfortunately, I probably have a better chance of winning Partero's case than Billy's. Unless, of course, a certain party is willing to settle some old score with a certain other party so that we can get some facts straight around here."

"I thought we were talking about this Partero case, not about some damned fool woman," Tom muttered. "Why don't you stick to the subject at hand?"

Kerry forced down a laugh. "Okay. Claudio Partero. He's able to identify the man who shot him. If we—I mean the state—can match the bullet with this

Greg Harvey's gun, they've got a pretty good case, wouldn't you say?"

"Oh, it's not that simple, Kerry."

"Why not? What do you mean, Tom?" Kerry wondered if Tip had already told him about his own investigation into the man at the gazebo. She knew that Tom was probably right, that things would not be as cut-and-dried as she envisioned them, but she was ready for the challenge.

"It's never simple," he told her, and she breathed a sigh of relief. Tom was just in one of his moods. "After all, what do we really know about this Partero guy? I mean, where is he from?"

"I already checked him out," she replied promptly. "He's got no record, and is exactly what he says he is. A musician who's been here for five years and can't get a job with the Boston Symphony Orchestra. He lives with his family in the North End."

"Why doesn't he get himself a North End lawyer, then?"

"Oh, so that's it!" Now she understood. "You don't want to take his case because he's not Avenue, is that it? Tom, you should be ashamed of yourself."

"Now why should I be?" he inquired querulously, although she knew he knew quite well.

"Are you telling me that you restrict your services to a client on the basis of his ethnic background?"

"Of course not! I've got plenty of Italian clients!"

"On the basis of where he lives, then? That doesn't sound kosher to me, Tom."

"Kosher smosher. I don't know the guy, that's all. And I think this case is not as much of a cinch as you're making it out to be, young lady. I think you've got yourself something juicy here, and you're not going to let it out of your sharp little teeth, are you?''

Now it was Kerry's turn to be defiant. "Why should I?''

Tom stared at her for a minute and then shrugged. "No reason, I guess. You're a good lawyer, Kerry, my girl, and I guess you've got your ambitions too. Just like my son. All you young people today..."

"Tip has nothing to do with this," she said too quickly.

Tom's bushy eyebrows rose. "I never said he did. I just said I hope you don't go rushing in over your head just because you've got something that appeals to your Florence Nightingale instinct.''

"Oh, you're a great one to talk. Aren't you the guy who takes cases for his old friends and charges them a beer or two for all your work? Huh, Sir Galahad?''

They grinned at each other, acknowledging their shared trait of sympathy for the underdog. "Well,'' Tom said, trying to sound more begrudging than he actually was. "I guess I'll go with your instincts on this one, Kathleen. I guess we'll take the case.''

"Like hell you will,'' came an angry voice from the doorway, and they both turned simultaneously to see Tip standing there.

Chapter Six

Tom and Kerry both turned to him, staring. "You want to explain yourself, young man?" Tom inquired curtly. Kerry knew he did not approve of anyone using "coarse" language in front of women, even if it was his son and the woman in question his employee, who he knew heard plenty of such language on Dorchester Avenue every day.

"I would very much like to explain myself," said Tip, striding in and taking a seat. He looked at Kerry, his dark eyes blazing. "But first I would like Kerry to do some explaining. Like how she managed to get herself hired by Mr. Partero for this fool's task?" He leaned back against the chair and crossed his arms imperiously over his chest, waiting for an answer.

Kerry's first thought, which she hastily suppressed, was how good he looked. He wore a lightweight tan suit with an elegant European cut that accentuated his broad shoulders and trim torso. Underneath was a crisp sky blue Oxford shirt in what looked like the softest cotton imaginable. She had a strong urge to reach out and stroke his chest to feel the play of muscle beneath the smooth material. It was about 95 degrees out, even in the office it wasn't much less than 80, and already Kerry's clothes were wrinkled and uncomfortably damp. But Tip looked as crisp as a new sheet of paper, and more desirable.

Then she got annoyed. She didn't like him marching into her office and demanding an explanation from her, as if she needed to explain herself to anyone aside from Tom. Nor did she like the way he glared at her with absolutely no trace at all of the tenderness he had seemed so eager to display only hours before. She made an effort to glare right back.

"First of all," she said coldly, "I resent your calling it a fool's task. My client and I have discussed the case carefully, and so have Tom and I. We all agree that the case is quite clear-cut. And in the second place—"

"Forget the second place," he interrupted brusquely. Then he turned to Tom. "Pop, did you actually agree to let her go through with this madness? You know what happens if they arrest Harvey on this? You know what it means?"

Tom looked stricken. Kerry knew he hated to be put in a position where he had to make a choice, especially when the choice involved her and Tip. Especially Tip. but he reacted admirably. "Now wait a minute, son. Don't you think you're moving a little fast here? I think we all need to do a little explaining.'' He tried to look stern as he faced his son. ''And I think it only fair that you go first since you seem to have all the facts at your disposal.''

''Your partner isn't doing too bad in that department herself.'' Despite the rancor in his tone, it was clear that Tip was making an effort to control himself. He took a deep breath, unfolded his arms and thrust them into his pants pockets, stretching out his legs to accommodate them. Kerry looked at a point above his head. ''Kerry knows that there's more to this case then meets the eye, Pop,'' he went on.

''If I do,'' Kerry retorted, ''it's no thanks to you or your chain-smoking friend, Detective Wykoff.''

''That'll do, Kerry, Tip. Now both of you calm down so I can make some sense out of this. We're not going to get anywhere with you two jumping down each other's throats.'' Tom spoke with authority, and both Kerry and Tip shifted uneasily in their chairs like reluctant children. ''All right, Son,'' Tom went on when he was satisfied that his edict had been followed, ''why don't you just start at the beginning?''

''You know some of this already, Pop. Remember that case we were discussing the last time I saw you? The one where we thought that fellow—you know who I mean—might be able to help us out?''

''I know what you mean.''

''I don't,'' mumbled Kerry sullenly but not loud enough for Tom to hear.

''Anyway, that's what we've been investigating out there on the Boston Common. Some of those fellows have apparently been using the little gazebo as a meeting area, you know, a drop. Anyway, I've been out there, working with some of the guys on the force and another fellow from the A.G.'s office, trying to get a handle on just who's involved in this whole thing. And, of course, hoping to pick up some hard evidence while we're at it.

"Then, along comes somebody and takes a potshot at Kerry's little violinist and gives us all a good run for our money. Of course, this shooting's got nothing to do with our fellows, or so we think, it just complicates things a little bit for everybody."

"Especially for Claudio Partero," Kerry couldn't resist tossing in and was rewarded by warning looks from both father and son.

"Just complicates things a little, that is," Tip went on, "until super sleuth here decides to take on the lions and institute civil charges against Harvey on her client's behalf."

Kerry stood up quickly. "How did you know? I haven't even filed the formal indictment papers yet."

Tip stood up as well. "That's what I'm here to ask you! How did you know about Greg Harvey?"

They both started talking at once and their voices grew louder and louder until Tom had to place his considerable bulk in their line of vision to stop them. "Hey! You kids better simmer down or I'll toss you both out on the street!"

Tip and Kerry shut their mouths at the same moment, aware that they had let their passions get the better of them.

"You'd think you two were an old married couple, the way you go at each other," Tom muttered and, sitting back down heavily, scowled at them both. "Look at you, like cats and dogs!"

Kerry and Tip met each other's eyes, and a glimmer of humor lit Tip's face. "It's amazing to think we just met, isn't it?" he deadpanned, and Kerry had to duck her head to avoid the blaze of intimacy she saw behind his smile.

"Yeah, it sure is," acknowledged Tom, looking sharply from one to the other. He was silent for a moment, then shook his head as if to clear from it an unwarranted thought. "Now, where were we? You were trying to explain something, weren't you, Tip?"

"Right. Anyway, I found out this afternoon from Stan Wykoff that not only has Kerry been to the hospital to see Partero, but she's managed to convince him to press civil charges against his assailant. And Harvey's been arrested on state's charges, too. You know what they are? Attempted murder!" He looked incredulously at his father and then turned to Kerry. "What I want to know first is how you got to see Partero."

"Remember that message from the hospital?" Kerry asked him.

"That was Partero calling you?"

"His brother."

Tip slapped his hand to his forehead. "I should have known." He shook his head. "And how exactly did Mr. Partero find you, may I ask?"

Kerry shrugged and tried to make her voice sound casual. "Simple. I just slipped my business card into his pocket while I was holding his head. Told him he could call me if he needed any help."

Tip sighed loudly. "Boy. Talk about ambulance chasing." But there was no more anger in his voice. Instead, she thought she detected a faint note of admiration. He even smiled as he mimicked her voice. "'You know how your father is always handing out business cards,'" he quoted. "Yeah, I know, all right."

Kerry smiled back. "Hey, a girl's got to make a living somehow, you know?"

They were both grinning broadly at each other, until Tom once again intervened. "If you two don't mind," he said testily, "I would appreciate your keeping the private jokes down to a minimum and going on with this—if you don't mind."

He looked suspiciously from one to the other until Tip managed to tear his eyes away from Kerry and spoke. "That's really all there is, as far as I know, Pop. Except, of course, you know what a civil charge against Harvey will do to our case. It means the criminal charges will get bullied right through the court. He'll be hauled off the streets and taken into custody, and he'll be tied up trying to beat this little rap, and we won't be able to get a thing on him or on his friends. It'll set *our* case back a good six months, if not more. If he goes to jail, we'll have to start from square one."

"But why? Why is Greg Harvey so important to your case? What about the other guys?" Kerry asked.

"Harvey's the only one we've got clear evidence on right now," Tip told her. "But it's not enough to do him any real damage, and we're leaving him out there so we can keep an eye on him and maybe pull in some hard evidence on his pals and his boss."

"Do you know who the boss is?"

"Oh, we know, all right. A guy by the name of Santos. We just can't touch him until we can link him up with Harvey. And we have to be real careful how we do it, or the whole thing could get thrown out of court. That's why I'm in there with Wykoff's boys. Just to make sure everything's done legally.''

Tom beamed at his son. "They're lucky they've got someone like you to work with them, my boy. Too many times, the police department sticks their feet where their mouths should be.''

"Thanks, Pop.'' Tip looked at Kerry, not at his father, as he replied.

"Well, then, I think that clears it up, don't you Kerry?''

Kerry turned to stare at Tom. Clearly, he expected her to drop the case now that she had heard Tip's argument. "Wait a minute. I don't think it's clear at all.'' She turned to Tip. "You're telling me that Greg Harvey is your only link to this big case you're working on, Tip? Are you also telling me that the state will refuse to consider my client's charges because your office needs Mr. Harvey on the streets to pursue their case?''

"No, I wouldn't tell you that at all,'' Tip replied judiciously. "After all, that would be an obstruction of justice.'' His eyes flashed dangerously. "We would never interfere with justice, of course. But I am telling you that the A.G.'s office has invested a lot of time and money in this very important matter, and the attorney general himself feels it would be a shame to lose Mr. Harvey to this smaller matter.''

"What about Claudio Partero's career as a violinist?'' Kerry asked softly. "Don't you think it would be a shame to lose that, too?''

For the first time, Tip appeared a little uncomfortable. "Of course that's a shame, Kerry. That's a tragedy. But taking Harvey to court isn't going to make Partero's shoulder sound again. And besides, you know the state is never going to get a full attempted murder conviction on the guy."

"First of all, I'd like to know how you found out they're going for the A.M. conviction? I wasn't even sure of that myself until I checked at City Hall."

Tip smiled. "I have my sources."

Kerry waved this pat answer off impatiently. "And second of all, I'd like to know why you don't think they'll get a conviction on an A.M. count. Do your sources include judges in high places, perhaps? Judges who might refuse to hand down an indictment on my case?"

Tip bristled. "Of course not. I just happen to know that they'd never get a jury to believe that shot was premeditated. At the most, they'll figure Harvey meant that shot for someone else, although they won't be able to prove who. So he'll get off on some sort of technicality, and then where will your friend Claudio be?"

"He's not my friend, he's my client. And what would you say if I told you that he could prove it wasn't an accident? That Greg Harvey shot at him on purpose?"

Tip's eyes widened and Tom's mouth dropped open. "You never said anything about this, Kerry," Tom complained, but Kerry ignored him to watch Tip's reaction.

"Are you serious?" he inquired softly. "Is that what Partero told you?"

"I'm afraid that's privileged information, Counselor," she replied haughtily.

"Privileged my foot," he shot back. "Do you know what this means, Kerry?"

"I know what it means," she snapped. "You don't need a Harvard degree to figure out what it means, Tip. It means Claudio isn't as dumb as everyone thinks he is."

He brushed off the remark with an imperious wave of his hand. "Do you realize the danger this would put Partero in? If he really does know something and thinks that Harvey shot him because of that, then he would really be crazy to press the case. Then everyone will *know* he knows something!"

"Obviously it's too late for that," she said coldly. "Or he wouldn't have been shot in the first place, now would he?"

"Kerry, be reasonable, for God's sake!"

"I *am* being reasonable. It's you who aren't seeing reason. You want Claudio Partero to just forget everything, so you and your pals don't have to worry about your precious case being fouled up in any way. So he should just go home and learn to play the fiddle with his foot, is that it?"

"Now you *are* being unreasonable. Don't you understand anything about the way the criminal mind works?"

"Don't condescend to me, Tip Sullivan. Just because I'm stuck here handling things like Mrs. Ranieri and Billy Stuart doesn't mean I don't know what goes on in the great big world of criminal justice. We do have a primitive idea of life down here on the Avenue, in case you've forgotten in your big rush to leave your father and get into the glamorous world up there on Beacon Hill!"

This speech was so scathing that it stunned even Kerry herself into an embarrassed silence. She had lost her temper and managed to insult both Tip and his father, not to mention having sounded like a jealous harpy into the bargain. She bit her lip and looked down to avoid their eyes. She was ashamed of herself yet knew that Tip had goaded her into it by acting as if she knew nothing at all. If he had that little respect for her as a lawyer, what must he think of her as a woman? she wondered. Her face burned with anger and humiliation.

But it was Tom who spoke first, in a voice that held more puzzlement than reproach. "What's going on here?" he inquired. "What's going on between you two?"

"Pop, do you think you could . . . if you'll just give me a minute alone with Kerry, I think maybe we can straighten this whole thing out. Do you think you could . . . ?"

"Sure, sure. I'll just run out and grab a bite at the pub. You two . . . you two talk, and I'll be back in a little while. That's a good idea." Tom's voice was filled with relief, and Kerry heard the door open and shut rapidly behind him.

She lifted her eyes and found Tip smiling down at her. "I figured he'd be itching to get out of here. This kind of thing really makes him uncomfortable."

"I know. I shouldn't have . . . blown up like that. I'm sorry."

"Oh, no, I didn't mean that!" he was quick to reply. "I deserved that. I mean being caught in the middle, you know. Tom can't stand it when he has to decide between two things he loves. Like whether to have a whiskey or a beer."

Kerry was forced to smile at the image Tip conjured of Tom, standing at the bar of the Gaelic and taking ten minutes to make up his mind. "This is a little different," she said softly.

"A little. It's a little more complicated. but let's not talk abut Tom right now. Let's talk about us."

He came around and sat on her desk very close to her chair. Again, his physical attractiveness exerted itself, and she had to struggle against the urge to stand up and press her body against the long length of his. "I don't know what there is to talk about," she murmured.

"There's plenty to talk about. I want to make it very clear to you, Kerry, that this whole thing has nothing to do with you and me—with us together, I mean."

She looked up, incredulous. "Are you serious? This has everything to do with us!" She was suddenly angry again, but it had nothing to do with the Partero case. "We're obviously on very different sides of the fence here, Tip, and I don't appreciate your powerplaying." She spread her hands on the table in front of her and examined them. "Besides, there's nothing going on between us besides this. I mean—"

She did not finish her sentence because his hands came down hard over hers. "Are you seriously trying to tell me," he inquired, "that you and I don't have any kind of a relationship?"

His eyes were penetrating into hers, and it was hard to avoid their demanding glitter. "A relationship? I run into you while you're involved in a stakeout. You pick me up, and we exchange a kiss or two. Then I get tangled up in your case, and you—" she bit her lip before going on "—you take me to bed, hoping to keep me busy so I won't mess up your case. That doesn't sound like much of a relationship to me."

Kerry didn't realize it until she'd said it, but that was at the core of her overreaction. Tip was wrong; the Partero case and Greg Harvey had everything to do with their relationship—whether they liked it or not. It had shaped it, formed it. It had been the reason for their night in bed together, if she were to be brutally honest with herself. And she had to accept the cold hard fact that Tip, for all his protestations to the contrary, would never have taken such an interest in her if it hadn't been for the crime at the gazebo. That, and her obvious availability had made her an easy mark.

But he seemed genuinely angry and, grabbing both her hands, pulled on them. "Look at me!" he demanded angrily. "Look at me when you say something like that." His tone softened when he saw the pain in her eyes. "Now look at me, Kerry, and try and tell me that you really believe what you just said, that what happened last night had to do with anything else in the world except you and me." His own eyes softened. "Try and tell me last night wasn't magic for you. If you can say it to my face, I'll believe you."

She stared at him and opened her mouth. Yes, she wanted to say. I know how men like you operate. You may not have known that it would be worth your while to take me to bed, but you weren't about to let the opportunity pass. At best, I'm probably just another notch on your gun. Pop's partner, just an interesting switch from your usual fare, I suppose.

Escape again ... with 4 FREE novels

That's right. We'll send you all 4 Silhouette Special Edition novels (a $10.00 value), plus a *Folding Umbrella and Mystery Gift FREE*. Take:

Lisa Jackson's DEVIL'S GAMBIT. Tiffany had problems with her breeding farm long before handsome Zane Sheridan offered to buy her out. What was it in his cold grey eyes that made Tiffany so uncertain? And so convinced?

Natalie Bishop's STRING OF PEARLS. Brittany and Devon were once devoted to one another. Now, circumstances have brought them together again, perhaps on opposite sides of the law.

Patti Beckman's DATELINE: WASHINGTON. Newspaper reporter Janelle Evans saw Bart Tagert only as a rival, until a Washington scandal brought them together—and into each other's arms.

Linda Lael Miller's STATE SECRETS. Holly Llewellyn's cousin was about to become President of the United States. Secret Service agent David Goddard's interest in her was strictly professional... or was it?

After you receive your FREE books, we'll send you 6 new books to preview every month for 15 days. If you decide to keep them, pay just $11.70 (a $15.00 value) with no extra charge for home delivery. You'll also receive the Silhouette Books Newsletter FREE with every book shipment. Cancel at any time, just by dropping us a note. The first 4 books, Folding Umbrella and Mystery Gift are yours to keep in any case.

Get a FREE
Folding Umbrella
& Mystery Gift too!

Escape with
4 FREE

**Silhouette Special Edition novels
(a $10.00 Value) and get a Folding
Umbrella & Mystery Gift, too!**

Silhouette Special Edition®

Silhouette Books, 120 Brighton Rd., P.O. Box 5084, Clifton, NJ 07015-9956

☐ **YES!** Please send me my four Silhouette Special Edition novels along with my FREE Folding
Umbrella and Mystery Gift, as explained in this insert. I understand that I am under no
obligation to purchase any books.

NAME _____
(please print)

ADDRESS _____

CITY _____ STATE _____ ZIP _____

Terms and prices subject to change.
Your enrollment is subject to acceptance by Silhouette Books.

Silhouette Special Edition is a registered trademark.

CES076

But she couldn't bring herself to say it. She knew, even as she opened her mouth, that it wasn't true. "I can't," she whispered, and he pulled her up against him and pressed her near to him and kissed her long and deep.

Kerry's first impulse was to resist, but that didn't last long. His arms wrapped around her back with such intimate familiarity, such a clear and perfect knowledge of what would feel right to her, that she could not refuse the pleasure. She made a small, muffled sound of protest that turned into a sigh as she settled herself across his breadth and leaned into his lips. She could feel the hardness of his perfect white teeth behind his soft lips, and every so often his tongue would search for hers and indulge in a moment's playful combat that would leave her with a sweet taste in her mouth and a line of goose bumps all the way down her spine.

His hands seemed to fit perfectly over the ridges of her back so that the fingertips could gently massage the edges of both breasts in small circles of delight that emanated forward until her nipples pressed erect against the smooth cotton of his shirt. She had been right about the shirt—it was at once immaculately crisp and impossibly soft to the touch. Kerry pressed her hands against his chest and slid them up and down, hungry for the feeling she had denied herself before.

She would have been content to let the embrace go on to its ultimate conclusion, to a replay of the ecstasy that his every touch recalled with almost painful clarity. But even Tip seemed to know that it was impossible, and that therefore it was imprudent to continue even for just a little while.

Reluctantly they pulled apart, making several false attempts that only ended in their lips meeting again with renewed passion. Finally just as Tip was leaning forward to find her mouth again with his, she managed to place her fingertips strategically between their lips.

"This is getting us nowhere fast," she said huskily.

"Actually, it's getting us somewhere," he replied ruefully, "and all too fast. But you're right. We'd better stop before we have the entire Avenue staring in through the windows."

They both glanced guiltily out through the glass and were relieved to find that no one had even paused in their travels to witness the scene. Kerry felt that her desire had been fairly shouted over the glass transom. Tip looked back at her and smiled.

"Your virtue is safe for the time being."

"It's hardly my virtue that I'm concerned about," she told him, feeling his arms slip slowly and reluctantly from around her back.

"What is it, then?"

"Tip, let's not go into this now, okay? We've got too many other issues to deal with. Please?"

"All right." He lifted one finger and tipped her chin up. "But I just wanted to prove to you, and to myself, that we are *not* dealing with a nonrelationship here. Far, far from it."

She had to admit that her earlier fears had been ungrounded. What she felt for Tip was still undefined and amorphous, but she could no longer pretend to herself that it did not exist at all or that it was not reciprocated in equal measure.

Kerry sat back down in her chair and Tip moved back to the seat he had occupied. Thus safely separated from each other by six feet of air space and a solid wooden desk, they attempted to resume their conversation.

"Tip," Kerry began with a sigh, " why did you come here this afternoon? Did you really think you could talk me out of taking on the Partero case?"

Tip sighed as well. "The honest-to-goodness truth? No. I mean, I was really hoping I could, and I still am, Kerry. Don't get me wrong."

She opened her mouth to make a retort, but he smiled and held up his hand. "No, come on, don't get all worked up again, Kerry. I'd be less than a good public servant if I didn't do what I felt was in the best public interest in this matter, and you know it." He shook his head. "But somehow, even as I managed to work myself up to a righteous rage on behalf of the Commonwealth of Massachusetts, a part of me was hoping that you would be what I thought you were: dedicated, committed—" he grinned "—and stubborn as all get out."

She was forced to grin back. "I guess I didn't disappoint you on any score, did I?"

"You came through with flying colors, believe me. But that doesn't mean you're right, you know. You're taking on something that might be too much for you, Kerry."

"How can you know what's too much for me?" she demanded. "You don't know the first thing about my skill as a lawyer!"

"Wait a minute. Wait a minute! This has nothing to do with your skill as a lawyer. First of all, I know my old man well enough to know he wouldn't be working with anybody but the best, and from what he's told me about your work, you're better than that. Secondly, anybody who has your fighting spirit has to be a scourge in the courtroom." He shuddered theatrically and Kerry chuckled.

"Yeah," she remarked dryly, "you should see me go after those scoundrels on parking meter violations. I'm a real Clarence Darrow, all right."

"So you don't get much chance to strut your stuff in municipal court. That's no reason to go and take on a case like this one, just to prove to the world that you can."

"That's not why I'm taking this case!" she said sharply. His words stung because they had the bite of truth to them—a truth she preferred to deny to both Tip and herself.

"Why are you taking it, then?"

"I'm taking it because it's important, because I feel that Claudio Partero deserves a little justice, a little revenge if you will, and because I see no reason for a man like Greg Harvey to go unpunished for this crime on the off chance that you might be able to pin him with another. Justice doesn't work that way, Tip, and you know it."

He looked sad. "Justice works in some very weird ways, believe me. I've seen it work where you'd be hard-pressed to find the justice no matter which way you looked at a case." He sounded briefly bitter but recovered quickly. "And in this case I think you'll find it will tie you and your client in particularly tight knots.''

"That doesn't matter, Tip. My job is to see that Claudio gets his chance to make his claim against Greg Harvey in court in front of a jury of his peers. I'm not in business to weigh the odds before I enter the arena. That's not what being a lawyer is all about to me. I can only state my case to the best of my ability and believe that what is right will prevail.''

She knew that her little speech sounded pompous, even to her ears, but Tip seemed to appreciate it. He ducked his head for a minute, and when he raised it again, his eyes were soft. "Bless you, Kathleen Sullivan. I really think you believe in that creed, and up where I work it's hard to come by someone who hasn't been made cynical enough to laugh at a sentiment like that, no matter how faithfully uttered.''

"And what about you, Tip? Have you been made cynical, too?'' She cocked her head and smiled. "I didn't hear you laugh.''

He shook his head. "Oh, I've been hit, too, don't think I haven't. It's just that I may have been hit a little less hard than some of my colleagues. Pop's legacy, I guess.''

"I guess.'' They smiled gently at each other.

"So,'' Tip said at last,'' I guess this means I can't persuade you to drop the case. Am I right?''

She looked at him evenly and nodded. "That's right.''

He nodded back. "But I'm warning you, Kerry. This isn't going to be easy, and it's going to be part of my job to see to it that it isn't. We need Greg Harvey,

and we're not going to let him get away without a
fight."

Kerry saw that he was perfectly serious, and despite
the warmth that still lingered in his eyes, she could
hear the cold determination in his voice. For the first
time, she felt a mild frisson of fear. "What does that
mean?" she asked, trying to sound unafraid.

Tip didn't answer right away but turned and stared
out the window, apparently lost in thought. She gazed
at his strong profile and chewed at her lower lip. Am
I doing the right thing? she asked herself. Am I doing
this because I believe in it or because I have to prove
something by it? It was a little of both, she had to admit, but she felt that her interest in Claudio out-
weighed her interest in the challenge of the case itself.
And besides, she reminded herself, being challenged
would only goad her on to better work.

But Tip's words of warning did not go unheeded.
She had not taken on the boys downtown before, and
she knew that Tip was right: sometimes justice could
be convoluted beyond belief, especially when there was
power to be gained in its execution.

"The first thing I'm going to do," said Tip suddenly, "Is try to convince Pop not to work with you on
the case."

Kerry was shocked. "You wouldn't!"

He turned slowly to face her. "I'm afraid I would,
Kerry. Without Pop, you're going to be missing a lot
of strong support. Maybe that'll make you think
twice."

Her mouth had dropped open. She had expected
determination, but not ruthlessness, and certainly not
so soon after she had been in his arms. She realized

that she had underestimated Tip Sullivan, and her fear grew stronger. But she was not about to let him see it.

"It won't," she snapped. "I could use Tom's help, but I won't be lost without it. And it won't be the first time I've won a case on my own merits."

"I'm sure it won't."

His constant switching from adversary to supporter was getting confusing. For the first time since he had appeared in the doorway, Kerry wished he would leave, wished that he had never shown up in the first place.

"Anyway," she said sullenly, "Tom'll never agree to that. He's already said he would help me, and he's a man of his word."

"We'll see about that." Tip rose as Tom walked through the door.

"Well," Tom said, looking brightly from one to the other, "have you two managed to work things out without tearing each other to pieces? Eh?" It was clear that "lunch" in the pub had done Tom good. He looked much better and less threatened by the altercation between Tip and Kerry. He even had a bright sparkle of amusement in his eyes as he surveyed them, which Kerry put down to his liquid meal.

"Actually, Pop, we've sort of left things up to you. We're going to let you decide what you think would be the right thing to do in this matter."

The smile disappeared. Tom looked hard at Tip and then turned to Kerry. "That so, Kathleen?"

"Not exactly, sir," Kerry said, keeping her eyes on Tom and avoiding Tip's. "I've already told Tip that I refuse to back off from this case. I don't think the attorney general's office has any business interfering in a criminal suit just because they haven't gotten their act together. And I don't think the state would dare refuse to hand down the indictment, because they know I'd blow the whistle if they did. Partero deserves the best counsel he can get, and I have every intention of giving it to him." She took a deep breath. "What you do is up to you, Tom."

The smile was replaced with a deep frown. "So. You've left it in my hands, is that it? I have to choose, am I right?"

"That's right, Pop." Tip's voice was cool and level.

"You can choose, Tom. I'm going to be handling the case regardless, but you can choose," Kerry put in.

Tom went over to his desk and sat down heavily, laying his hands on his knees and looking from one to the other as if he expected to find the answer written on his palms. "You realize," he asked, lifting his head, "what you're asking me to do here, don't you? What you're asking me to choose?"

Neither Tip nor Kerry answered. They both knew perfectly well what they were asking: that Tom chose between his loyalty to his job and his partner, and his love for his son. The room was silent and Kerry concentrated on the occasional drip from the air conditioner in order to avoid listening to the thudding of her heartbeat. She knew that she would have to stick to her determination despite Tom's decision, but she also knew that if he withdrew his support, she would be sorely in need of advice—and would have nowhere to get it. Tom's sharp legal skills and street smarts were an unbeatable combination, and would come in especially handy in a case like this where wits were as important as brains.

She also had to ignore a sharp stab of pity for Tom, who had probably been dreading and working to avoid just such a confrontation as this one for many years. He had probably known it would come to this one day, his Avenue loyalties and populist principles of justice versus those of his upscale son. But she could not bear to watch his discomfort as he tangled with the problem at last. Nor could she capitulate to make things easier for him.

It seemed as though hours had dragged by without any of them moving. Finally Tom looked up. He looked first at Kerry, and she was sure he was going to tell her that she was on her own. But, after giving her a long, hard stare that she was unable to read, he turned to Tip.

"I'm sorry, son. My hands are tied on this one. I've already told Kerry I'd be there for her, and you know I can't go back on my word. Besides—" he looked down, almost as if he was ashamed to face Tip as he said it "—I kinda feel that she's right. I know it's gonna be hard and that we're fighting an uphill battle against city hall, but I've gotta do what's right. And if Kerry really feels we should go after this Harvey guy for her client, then I'm gonna have to go with her." He stopped and swallowed, and Kerry thought she had never seen him so uncomfortable. "You understand, don't you, son?" he pleaded softly. If she had dared, Kerry would have jumped up and kissed the old man.

Tip pursed his lips and smiled ruefully. "Of course, Pop. I understand." He laughed sadly and shook his head. "To tell you the truth, I never expected anything different." He stood up and ran his hands down his already perfectly pleated pants. Kerry looked away and swallowed.

"Well, I guess I've made my case pretty clear, and so have you." He looked at Kerry for the first time since Tom had come in. "Good luck to you, Counselor. You're gonna need it." He did not smile as he said it, and Kerry felt her heart rising into her throat.

At the door, Tip turned and smiled at last, but it was not a reassuring look. "See you in court," he said tersely, and was gone.

Kerry stared at the door after him, hoping she would not let the tears she felt stinging her eyes bubble over. She was trying to remind herself that Tip was only doing his job, just as she was only doing hers. She was trying to remind herself of what he had told her, that none of this had anything to do with their relationship, and that she had believed deeply in his kisses only a few moments before. She was trying to remind herself that he was incapable of a treachery so deep, that her instincts about him and her feelings for him were sound.

She also had to thank Tom, but when she turned to him, gratitude written all over her face, he raised his hand and shook his head to ward it off. "Don't say it," he told her. "Don't say a word."

"Okay," she replied gently. "I won't."

"Good, because you and I have a lot of work to do, and we can't spare a second for any mushy platitudes."

Kerry felt better just hearing Tom his old gruff self. "You're right," she said briskly, pulling a clean legal pad and a sharp pencil from her desk drawer. "So where do we start?"

"First things first," said Tom, looking at her sharply. "Let's see..."

"What? We've got to file the formal brief, interview Claudio again, talk to any witnesses, get the police report, find out who the judge is...so what's first?"

"The first thing you do," Tom said portentously, "is find yourself something suitable to wear to court. You can't show up looking like somebody's secretary or something. Go out and buy yourself a suit, so you look like a real lawyer. *That's* first."

Chapter Seven

She went to Filene's with Marie that very night to shop for a suit. She wasn't taking Marie along for advice—her taste in clothes was far from Kerry's and farther still from what Kerry knew she would need for court—but for company and moral support, and the chance to be with someone who wasn't involved in her immediate dilemma.

But Marie was no help at all. She was avid for every detail of the crime that Kerry had witnessed and eager to pry out any inside information she could on the progress of the case. It was hard to maintain a professional distance from someone like Marie, who could have made a top secret spy-ring scandal sound like just so much neighborhood gossip.

"I mean it, Marie, I can't tell you. That's privileged information between lawyer and client. You know that."

"Aw, come on. You mean you can't tell your old pal Marie the name of the guy he's pressing charges against?" Marie spread her hands across her ample hips. She was clothed tonight in bright blue cotton cropped pants beneath a red-and-white-striped sailor top that revealed a lot of non-sailorlike cleavage. "But that's ridic! I mean, everybody and their uncle's gonna find out about it in the papers as soon as you file."

"That's true. And as soon as we file, everybody and their uncle is welcome to the news. But until then my hands are tied. Believe me."

Marie followed Kerry up the subway stairs onto the main floor of Filene's. The huge room was filled with bright summery colors and the clashing scents from the perfume counter, but at least it was cool. Kerry stopped to finger a soft challis shoulder wrap in pale pink and green. "No," she muttered to herself, "that's not suitable at all." And she moved on.

"I'll bet I know who it is," chattered Marie, barely aware of her surroundings, so absorbed was she in the matter at hand. "I'll bet it's that creep Larry Riley. You know, the one who beat up the guitar player who was playing for quarters in the subway last fall?"

"Nope. Not Larry Riley."

"Then it must be Ace Carson, the guy they're always kicking out of the Gaelic for singing Irish songs so loud no one can hear themselves think. I'll bet this violinist just interfered with old Ace's serenade, and he..."

"Nope. Not Ace Carson, either."

"It's not Ace Carson either? Then who the—Hey, where are you going?"

They had reached the escalators, and instead of heading down to the basement level where they usually went, Kerry headed upstairs.

"I'm going to Investments."

"Investments? You planning to buy some stock in this place or something?"

Kerry giggled. "No, silly. I mean Investments dressing. That's where all the Boston professional women buy their suits."

"Whew!" Marie made a face. "You really are going all out for this thing, aren't you? It must be some big deal for Sullivan and Sullivan."

"It's a big deal to me," Kerry said softly.

Marie put a gentle hand on her arm. "I know it is, honey. I can tell you're going all out, and I just want you to know I know you'll do fine. I know how much it all means to you."

Kerry patted Marie's hand. "Thanks, pal. I needed that." They emerged on the fourth floor and entered the Investments section, where muted music and chic mannequins set the subdued tone.

"That's not all you're gonna need," Marie whispered. "You're gonna need a major bank loan to finance one of these."

Kerry chuckled as she reached out and fingered a pale jade tweed jacket with deep green velvet on the collar and cuffs. "Oooh, look at this! Isn't it gorgeous!" She lifted the sleeve and turned over the price tag. "My God!" she breathed. "You're not kidding!"

Marie looked over her shoulder and whistled softly through her teeth. "Come on," she said, tugging on

Kerry's shirt. "Let's go back down to the basement where we belong."

But Kerry set her jaw and shook her head. "Nope. If I'm going to do this, I'm going to do it right. I have to have the right attitude when I go into that court-room, and to have the right attitude you need the right clothing." She pulled the suit off the rack and held it up against her chest. "Think of it as a uniform, Ma-rie. Or as armor. If I go in there armored in a suit like this, I'll have extra protection against those lean and hungry wolves in the A.G.'s office."

"I know one lean and hungry wolf I wouldn't mind getting attacked by," Marie observed with a broad wink. "And I was under the impression that you had already been bitten."

Kerry chose to ignore the remark. "In a basement suit, no matter how chic, I'll know I'm in a basement suit. And that'll be a chink in my armor, don't you see?"

"But no one else'll know. You could probably get the same suit downstairs for half the price, less, maybe!"

"Ah," said Kerry, inspecting herself in the mirror. "But that's the whole point. I intend to pay full price for this affair. Pay full price, and get my money's worth, every cent." The pale green color suited her fair hair and tawny skin and brought out the green flecks in her eyes. Then she remembered the price and, with a sigh, hung the suit back on the rack. "Maybe I can find something a little more . . . conservative."

"A little more cheap, you mean," Marie remarked candidly. "And I'd watch what I was doing if I were you. Paying full price for an affair can be pretty costly, believe me. I should know. I've paid full price several times over for a couple of mine."

Kerry rolled her eyes. "I wasn't talking about that kind of affair. I mean the court appearance, my client's case, the whole thing." She flicked through the racks and chose a dark gray wool herringbone with a black skirt.

"Oh, so you mean Tip Sullivan's got nothing to do with it, is that it?"

Kerry was looking in the mirror again. "That's what he says. This is strictly business, and I intend to be strictly business when I go in there Wednesday morning. I think I'm going to try this one on," she observed. "It'll look nice and neat with a white pleated shirt." She winked at Marie. "And it's half the price of the first one."

Marie followed her into the dressing room and watched with folded arms while Kerry put on the suit. It fit her perfectly. "What do you think?" she asked.

"What do I really think, or what do I think you want me to think?" inquired Marie.

Kerry made a face. "Marie, have you ever said less than what you really think?"

Marie raised her lavishly plucked brows. "I think you look like an undertaker. I wouldn't trust you with a parking ticket in that thing. Besides, it's August. You'll pass out in that wool shroud."

Kerry sighed and began to remove the suit. "You're right. I look awful. Go out there and see if you can find me something better."

Marie brought back a series of the worst suits available, and Kerry was really beginning to despair, when a pale and languid saleswoman handed in a beauty. It had a soft dusty rose linen jacket in a pretty herringbone pattern and a charcoal linen skirt with little flecks of color in it. The jacket's rather severe tailoring offset the feminine color, and the narrow skirt was flared just enough to show off Kerry's slim legs without being constricting. It fit like a glove, and imparted an air of chic but understated elegance even in the narrow confines of the dressing room.

"It's perfect for you," the saleslady observed approvingly. Kerry turned to Marie, who pursed her lips.

"I gotta admit, it looks pretty terrific. Now if you can manage to keep an iron in your briefcase, you'll be just fine."

The saleslady shot Marie a comtemptuous glance, and Kerry seized the moment to take a quick look at the price tag. It wasn't as expensive as the green tweed, but quite a bit more than the gray and black. She looked back at her reflection in the mirror. "I'll take it," she said impulsively.

"Good idea," said the saleswoman, and promptly disappeared.

"Sure, why not?" queried Marie when she had gone. "What's a month's salary among friends?"

It wasn't quite a month's salary, but Kerry was glad when she walked into the district courtroom Wednesday morning that she had spent the money. It wasn't that the room was impressive, far from it. The ceilings were high and the windows trimmed in ornate woodwork, but the pale green walls defeated the stately ceiling, and years of peeling paint and lack of washing had left the windows barely transparent. The floor was covered with linoleum in alternating green and gray squares flecked with yellow and scuffed with use.

Nevertheless, she felt that her "armor" had paid off. Because, sitting in the long benches behind the counselors' tables was a full complement of well-dressed, well-groomed men, sitting shoulder to shoulder and looking like a color spectrum which ran only from blue to gray—the attorney general's office all present and accounted for. Even Jason Cromack, the assistant A.G., was there. And at a preliminary hearing for a civil suit, yet. She felt a small thrill of importance ruffle her composure. A lot hung on her performance this morning—the criminal *and* civil suit as well as Claudio's future—and her own.

Kerry felt she was playing it right, right from the start. She timed her entrance, with Claudio walking beside her, pale and frail and wrapped heavily in gauze from neck to waist, so that everyone else in the room was already sitting. As a matter of fact, she waited until the moment just after the bailiff had checked his watch and the phalanx of men were beginning to shift impatiently in their well-cut jackets.

She made it a point not to look directly at Tip as she walked in, but it was impossible not to see him sitting there at the end of the line, looking impeccable in a lightweight dark blue suit. His hair gleamed like a dark gold beacon, and she averted her eyes, setting her gaze instead upon the moldy-looking stuffed eagle that occupied a place of honor over the American flag behind the judge's bench.

Fortunately the tall ceilings and operative ceiling fans kept the room nice and cool, so her linen suit looked and felt as she knew it should. Crisp, clean, authoritative. She and Tom had talked a long time about what tack she should take for this all-important preliminary hearing. This was the point at which the judge would decide whether to hand down an indictment against Greg Harvey. If Kerry played it right, Harvey would be tried by a jury and the state would proceed with the criminal prosecution. So, even if she won this battle, the war would by no means be in her hands.

Still, as Tom always said, the most important moment in any trial came in the first five minutes, when judge, counsel, accuser and accused faced one another for the first time. In that moment, Tom said, it was possible to predict the final outcome of any case simply by gauging the players' reactions to one another. Although Kerry had never been able to do so herself, she tended to trust Tom in all matters such as this.

Tom had judged that she should be the one to make the grand entrance, that she should take the reins as soon as she walked in. He had even declined to sit at the counsel table with her, but she saw him now, out of the corner of her eye, sitting in the second row behind the barrier, noting her demeanor—and her suit—with cautious approval.

Style wasn't the only matter they had discussed at length. Kerry felt well prepared for any contingency. She had gone over Claudio's testimony with him time and time again, and they both knew exactly what she would ask him and what he would answer. In a preliminary hearing, what one didn't say was as important as what one said, so they had worked long and hard on possible cross-examination questions, too, until Kerry and Claudio were convinced that they knew their material cold.

Even so, she had stayed up all night the night before, despite Tom's admonition that she get plenty of rest, going over her argument again and again. She had tried to anticipate every possible objection, defensive maneuver and bargaining tactic that the defense attorneys would throw at her and had carefully plotted all possible reactions and countermoves like a chess player playing an entire game in her head. The two defense lawyers were court appointed; apparently Greg Harvey and his cronies had not thought it necessary to use their own hired counsel for such an insignificant case—a fact that had not been lost on Kerry. She knew both lawyers by reputation. They had been handpicked by someone—the attorney general himself, perhaps?—and they were good. Very good.

Still, she knew she had made the right impression by the silence that fell over the room when she and Claudio entered. She walked over to the table, snapped open her briefcase and stacked her papers neatly in front of her. She nodded curtly to the defense table, whispered a few words of encouragement to Claudio, who had begun to grow increasingly nervous as the appointed time drew nearer, and then looked expectantly at the bailiff. She assumed that no one in the room, with the possible exception of Tom, would realize that she was as nervous as she had been when she had presented her first case; maybe more so.

A few moments later the judge arrived. Tom had found out his name beforehand and had told Kerry that the man had a reputation for being hard but fair. Kerry stood along with the rest of the court and hoped that nobody could see her heart pounding against her chest. She took a deep breath, swallowed twice and cast a glance back over her shoulder at Tom, who gave her an encouraging nod. The judge spoke a few words to the bailiff, sifted through some papers and then, peering over his glasses, told Kerry to present her case.

Considering the amount of effort she had put in preparing for this moment and the anxiety she had suffered, it was all a lot easier than she had expected it to be. The words came easily to her and in clear order, and the entire procedure seemed to go exactly according to the script she and Tom had worked out. First, Kerry described her client's occupation and skill and then the extent of his injury, all of which was corroborated by sworn statements she had gathered hastily from the Boston City Hospital doctors and a few well-known musicians who had heard Claudio play.

Then she explained that Claudio had been a victim of circumstance, forced to make his living in a spot that was known to be frequented by criminals, some of whom carried guns. This was met by an objection from the defense that was overruled by the judge, who said that since it was a matter of police record that a gun had been used at the scene of the crime and that a crime had been committed in the shooting of Claudio Partero, it was safe to say that a criminal had been carrying a gun on the scene. Kerry allowed herself a small gloat on that one—she had purposely been careful to avoid being overly specific, and it had paid off.

She went on to describe how Claudio had seen Greg Harvey's gun, and how, although he had not seen the shot actually being fired, he could place Harvey in the area from which it had been fired. She had a witness report testifying that a man who loosely fit Greg Harvey's description had been seen running from the area, which corroborated Claudio's testimony. She pointed out that, although the actual weapon had not been found, ballistics tests matched the bullet from Claudio's wound with the type of gun registered to Harvey. The only thing she did not mention was the fact that Claudio believed he knew the motive for the attack. That, as she and Tom had both agreed, was not necessary at this point in the proceedings and was better left unsaid until absolutely necessary.

The defense worked very hard in their client's behalf. They insisted that he had only been passing by the gazebo at the time of the attack and that the fact that a gun similar to the one that had been used on Claudio was registered in his name was purely circumstantial. They made a strong point for the fact that Harvey had no motive for shooting the violinist, but the judge was not convinced.

"I think," he said without taking much time for deliberation, "that there is enough evidence for this case to be remanded to the higher court to be tried by jury. We'll set a court date for . . . two weeks from today." He jotted it down and looked up. "Defendant is to be held on seventy-five-thousand dollars bail. Anybody come forward to pay that yet?"

"Not yet, your honour," said one of the defense attorneys. "But we expect . . ."

"Well, I don't care what you expect. Defendant can go to Charles Street if it looks like he's going to be bailed out soon. Otherwise we'll have to send him to Concord to await trial."

The defense attorneys took this bad news without a show of defeat, which was proper form for a professional, but Greg Harvey was not so sanguine. He looked wildly around the room, as if hoping that help would come from somewhere. Apparently he didn't see any possibilities, because he scowled and whispered something fiercely to one of the lawyers. The lawyer said something to calm him down, and the bailiff came to take Harvey to jail. Claudio had been instructed not to look at the defendant unless he absolutely had to, and Kerry decided it was good that he was looking the other way when Greg Harvey passed him, because the look he gave the musician was filled with fury.

"Well, well," said Tom behind them. "It looks like you pulled that one off without a hitch. Congratulations, Kerry."

"Thanks, Tom." Kerry felt the glow of victory, even though she knew perfectly well that this was only a small initial battle. But, when she stood up to shake his hand, she found that her knees were weak and she sat back down.

"Miss Sullivan," Claudio began.

"Please. You can call me Kerry," she said, smiling.

"Kerry. I can't thank you enough. It went exactly as you said it would. We didn't even have to testify."

"Don't thank me yet, Claudio. This was the easy part, believe me."

It was only when she had sufficiently recovered to be sure that her knees would not buckle again that Kerry allowed herself to turn around and look for Tip. She could see most of the men from downtown, including Detective Wykoff, who was standing and talking to one of the defense lawyers, but Tip was nowhere to be seen.

She wasn't sure whether to feel disappointed or relieved. "Come on, Claudio," she said, helping her client to his feet. "We'd better get you back home before your mother has my scalp. You have to go back to the hospital for more X rays this afternoon, don't you?"

She and Tom led Claudio down the hall to the back exit of the district courthouse, where his family was waiting for him. On the way, Tom saw one of his old cronies and excused himself to talk to him.

So Kerry and Claudio were alone when Tip accosted them in a narrow alcove off the hall, just before they got to the double doors that led outside.

"Just a minute," he said, stepping from the shadows and making both of them jump. Kerry had a sudden premonition of fear on her client's behalf and, clutching his good arm protectively, pulled him a bit behind her. Then she realized who it was.

"No, I'm not one of Greg Harvey's accomplices," Tip said, smiling thinly and stepping forward. "I just wanted to congratulate you on your performance in there just now. You did everything exactly the way you should have. Tom must be proud of you."

"I'm proud of myself," she replied defensively. Despite his suave smile, something in Tip's demeanor warned her that he was not there merely to praise her.

"I'm proud of her, too," said Claudio staunchly.

"That's good," said Tip. "That's very good, to have such confidence in your lawyer. Because you're going to need it."

Kerry knew then exactly what Tip was planning to do. "Come on, Claudio. Your brothers said they'd be waiting right outside. Let's get you to that car so you can go home and rest."

"That's a good idea," Tip said smoothly, "to have someone with you all the time. It's not advisable to be alone when you're involved in something like this."

"In something like what?" Despite Kerry's efforts to pull him away, Claudio was caught up in Tip's ruse. "What do you know about all of this? Who are you, anyway?"

"Claudio, forget it. He's just trying to scare you, and you mustn't listen to him. He's from the attorney general's office, and—" she cast a venomous look at Tip "—he's only doing his job."

"But what does he have to do with me? I want to know what you're talking about, mister!"

"Hasn't Kerry told you? Our office has been investigating Greg Harvey and his associates. Not a very savory bunch, as you must know."

"Claudio, I told you all that. Now don't worry about it, just come and get into the car."

"So you think I'm in danger, is that it? Are you trying to warn me off or something, or are you just trying to make it harder on us?"

"You should decide that for yourself, Mr. Partero," Tip said. "As long as your lawyer has informed you fully of the seriousness of your situation then the decision is yours to make, of course."

"She told me. She told me all about what you guys are looking for. But do you think there's really going to be trouble? Do you know something we don't know? Because my family—"

"Claudio!" Kerry's voice was authoritative enough to make him turn to her. She saw the fear in his eyes, and tried to calm her own fury enough so that she could speak calmly to him. "Now listen to me, Claudio. I've told you before, there is nothing to worry about on that score. You saw what happened in that courtroom today, it was just like Tom and I said it would be. The A.G.'s office couldn't stop the judge from sending the case to trial. Nobody is going to show up to bail Harvey out—they're going to feed him to the wolves and save their own skins. Nobody from that gang wants to come forward and implicate themselves by getting involved in this case. They have enough problems of their own. Greg Harvey is all alone, and this man is just trying to scare you so he can have Harvey back on the streets. He couldn't get what he wanted from the judge, so he's trying to get it from you. You don't want to give him Harvey, do you?"

Claudio looked at her and was silent for a long moment, struggling with his fears. Both Tip and Kerry were waiting to see what he would say.

"You're right," he said at last, his voice soft and controlled. "Of course you're right, Kerry. Let's go."

Kerry started to walk alongside Claudio through the doors. "Good try, Tip," she called over her shoulder. "Good try, but not good enough!"

Tip did not answer her taunt. "Think about it, Partero," he called out instead. "Think about it. Your lawyer is in over her head. I'd hate for you to get caught by her grandstanding tactics. It's not worth it, believe me."

Kerry and Claudio did not say a word to each other until he was safely ensconsed in the car. Then he leaned his head out the window and smiled up at Kerry's pale face. "Don't worry about that man," he told her, patting her hand as it rested on the car door. "He doesn't scare me. And I don't believe a word he says. Really, I don't. I believe it is worth it, and I believe in you."

Claudio's confidence was both touching and reassuring, but Kerry was not comforted by it. As soon as she could she went back home, changed out of her expensive suit and into a pair of shorts and a T-shirt and took the Red Line subway to Carson Beach. She had to get away from the courthouse, the office and from everyone who was connected with either. Even Marie would not provide any relief, not with her insatiable curiosity. Kerry had to be alone.

It was late afternoon by the time she got there, and most of the mothers who had spent the day with their small children were already packing them up and heading for home. Carson Beach was in a working-class neighborhood and had little natural beauty to recommend it to those who could afford to go farther away for relief from the heat. The shoreline looked out onto the busy Boston Harbor, with its airport and oil refinery, and the signs of crowded urban living were impossible to ignore. But the island—really a peninsula connected by a short bridge—had a large pentagonal stone fortress surrounded by grass and trees. From there the sea breeze blew in cool salty gusts, and if one walked all the way out to the far side of the fortress, it was possible to imagine that the city was not breathing down one's neck.

It was here that Kerry came to sit and think, as far as she could get without a car and on her limited budget from the realities that were plaguing her. But this afternoon she found no respite in staring out at the ocean tankers and fantasizing about going to some faraway port, or in watching the jumbo jets and planning a trip around the world. This afternoon, all she could think about was Tip.

Tom had warned her in his offhand and roundabout way that Tip would follow through on his promise to make things more difficult for them. "He's a man of commitment," he had said, shaking his head a trifle sadly. "He knows what his job is and what he has to do, and nothing stops him if he believes he's right. I guess he got it from his mother, that devout determination." He had paused, his eyes faraway. "I've learned not to take it personally," he'd said without much conviction. Then he had looked sharply at her. "And I hope you don't, either."

At the time, Kerry had had it on the tip of her tongue to insist that she had no reason to take it personally, but now she was glad she hadn't bothered. For one thing, Tom would probably not have believed her. He seemed to have intuited the depth of her relationship with his son, and although he had said nothing about it, she'd known better than to bring the subject up herself.

Besides, it no longer seemed very important. Tom had been right; Tip was pursuing his objective with devout determination. And Tom had been right about something else; Kerry was taking it very personally indeed.

It was impossible not to. After all, Tip had practically accused her of incompetence and self-serving motives, and in front of her client! He had frightened Claudio, although he had shrewdly stopped just short of saying anything that could be construed as a threat.

Kerry knew that she had to consider what Tip had said as carefully as she was considering the fact that he had said it. After all, she did have her client's best interests to consider, and there was the possibility that Tip was right—that Claudio would be endangered if he pursued the case. But she and Tom had talked that issue through many times and had come to the conclusion that Greg Harvey was no threat to Claudio simply because Harvey was no threat to his colleagues as long as the charges against him remained unrelated to the activities of the crime ring. And the fact that no one had appeared to post bail for him proved that they had been right.

But Kerry knew that the A.G.'s office was still not ready to sacrifice Greg Harvey to what they saw as a petty issue, and she knew that it would not be any easier when they got to trial. For the time being, Claudio was safe, but as soon as it was known that he believed he had been shot on purpose, things could get very sticky. And, if the A.G.'s office found out about that before the trial, they could haul Claudio in as a witness themselves, effectively destroying the momentum of his case against Greg Harvey.

It was all very complicated and would probably get more so. Yet the thing that kept welling up in Kerry's mind like an unshed tear was the fact that it had been Tip who had done the dirty work and Tip who would continue to haunt her, trying as hard as he could to make it more difficult for her to proceed. She had no doubt that he had tried to convince the judge not to hand down the indictment.

She knew he had said not to take it personally, but she was unable to convince herself that it was not personal. After all, Tip could easily have given the job to someone else in his office. And, after her victory in the preliminary hearing, there had been no reason for him to go after her and attack her credibility as a lawyer. It was almost as if *he* were taking it personally, as if he were offended that she should undertake to thwart his efforts.

Of course, she reasoned with herself, Tip Sullivan was a man who was used to having things done his way. He was not used to being crossed by an upstart female lawyer from Dorchester Avenue, and especially not when that lawyer worked in his own father's firm!

Still, none of that was any comfort at all. He had made it quite clear that he was not going to back off, and Kerry was quite sure that their relationship, whatever that had been, would be the first thing to be sacrificed. Already, the damage was irreparable. How could she even think about being with him again, about smiling into those warm eyes, about kissing those lips and being held in those strong arms, after what he had done to her today?

And yet she did think about that, until she could see nothing else before her but an image of Tip, naked and arching above her, his face transported by ecstasy. And no matter how hard she tried to work herself up into a righteous rage, that image kept reappearing with awful clarity until she was ready to weep with sheer frustration.

"All right," she said to herself as the sun began to throw long shadows across the gray granite of the old fortress. "I have to admit to myself that I'm infatuated with him. And why shouldn't I be, after all, he's been held up as an idol to me ever since I came to work for Tom! So, I'm fascinated, drawn...and seduced by the pleasure he gives me. Yes. But that doesn't mean I have to let it take control of my life. I can stick to my guns just as rabidly as he can stick to his. By the time this trial is over with, we'll probably be thoroughly disgusted with each other's firm principles, personal or not personal. We'll probably hate each other by then!"

Thus armed with fatalistic resolve, Kerry started to walk back toward the subway stop across the bridge. She was walking westward, facing the Boston skyline, which stood in sharp relief against the setting sun. She walked along the flagstone causeway gazing dreamily at the skyscrapers in the distance and feeling the sea wind lift the short hairs at the nape of her neck. The causeway was empty except for the lone figure of a man who walked in the opposite direction, toward her. Kerry did not notice him until he was close enough to be seen in silhouette.

She couldn't believe her eyes. *I must be imagining it,* she thought. The image she had taken such pains to banish from her mind's eye seemed to have taken on bodily form: she saw Tip walking toward her. "No," she said under her breath. *This is really too much.* The sun was in her eyes, and it was impossible to see the man's features, and she was alternately sure it was Tip, and sure she was imagining him. Then he spoke. "Kerry!"

Kerry obeyed her first impulse and turned and began walking the other way, away from him. This was the last thing she needed, she thought, to come face to face with him after having spent the afternoon trying to rid herself of his image. But he started walking faster to catch up with her, and she increased her pace as well, until they were both practically running back toward the edge of the island.

He caught her against the iron railing that separated the fort from the rocky beach below. "Hey, Kerry! What the hell are you doing, running away from me like that?" He swung her around to face him.

Suddenly all the anger she had been unable to summon that afternoon blew up inside her. He stood there, still perfect in his navy blue suit, not a hair out of place, a concerned look on his face. Kerry shook herself out of his grasp with a fierce shudder.

"What am I doing? What do you think I'm doing? I don't want to see you, Tip Sullivan! I don't want to see you or hear your voice!"

"Kerry, I . . ."

"Don't you think you've done your job well enough for the day? Don't you think you made your point this morning when you accosted my client and me in the hall? Or did your boss send you out here to do a little more hatchet work on me, since you couldn't buy off the judge?"

"Kerry, please . . ."

"How does it feel to attack a person you've just made love to, Tip? Tell me, because I'm really curious to know. I mean, I know it didn't mean all that much to you—"

"That's not true!" His eyes narrowed dangerously.

"—and I know it was all in the line of duty, but I'd like to know, exactly how do you manage it?"

"Stop it, Kerry."

The warning in his voice was clear, but Kerry was beyond caring. She was shaking with rage. "I mean, did the attorney general himself tell you how to handle this one? Did he tell you to come out here and draw a little more blood? Are you just following orders, or is this a bit of your own initiative? Maybe the whole thing was all planned out in that big, leather-lined office on Beacon Hill. Did he pick you especially because you're so skilled at the job? 'Hey, Sullivan, you're good at this. Go out there and seduce that little lady lawyer and then give her hell!'"

"I said stop it!" Tip grabbed her shoulders and shook her once, hard. Kerry was shocked into silence. Tip's face was pale and drawn with fury. "Stop it this minute, do you hear me?"

She did not reply, but clamped her mouth shut angrily. She had already said more than enough. Tip did not continue shaking her, but held on to her shoulders until he was sure she would not run away. He took several deep breaths to compose himself before he spoke. "I didn't come out here to attack you."

"Yeah. I suppose you came out here to apologize. How did you know I'd be here, anyway?"

"I asked Marie Cormier where you usually went when you wanted to be alone. She said she had no idea, but gave me a list of five possibilities." A small smile played briefly at the set line of his mouth. "This was number five. And I didn't come out here to apologize.''

''I'll have to remember to thank Marie,'' Kerry remarked sarcastically.

The smile disappeared, and for a moment Tip seemed to be considering turning around and walking away. He looked away from her, his expression hooded and brooding. Kerry felt her anger melting and struggled to hold on to it. Anger was her only weapon against her attraction to him.

''So if you didn't come out here to harass me, and you didn't come to apologize, why go to all the trouble? I mean, what else have we got to say to each other?''

He looked at her then, and his eyes melted into pools of sadness. He shook his head and reached into his pocket. ''I came to show you this,'' he said, producing a folded piece of stationary.

Kerry took it, thinking it was probably a court order or something, reversing the judge's decision. They got Greg Harvey released and there'll be no trial after all. She was so certain that the missive contained bad news of that sort that she had to read it twice before it made sense to her. ''What...what is this?'' she asked.

''It's a letter of resignation,'' he said tonelessly. ''I'm handing it in to the A.G. tomorrow morning. I've taken myself off the case.''

For a moment she didn't understand. ''But... why?''

''Why?'' He shouted the word angrily, causing a nearby flock of feeding sea gulls to leap noisily into the air. ''Because I'm in love with you, you idiot. That's why! Because I can't do my job and still be in love with you, and it's easier to quit than to stop the way I feel!''

He actually took a few angry steps away from her and then wheeled back to continue. ''This has never happened to me before in my life. Do you understand that? I am unable to function the way I should! I tried and I just can't keep it up! Unable to function, do you hear me? And it's all your fault!''

He stood there shuddering for a moment and then turned and began to walk away. She could feel his defeat, his immense anger and pain emanating even from a distance. Yet, even so, it took her a few moments to realize what had happened, what was happening and what she must do.

''TIP!'' She had to call his name very loudly because he was quite far away by the time she came to her senses. He turned and faced her, and she saw the indecision and the hope on his face even at that distance. She wanted to shout something out to him but felt that they had both done enough shouting for one day. So instead she began to run...to run toward him, gaining speed and elation as she went so that, by the time she reached him, she was both laughing and crying as he swept her into his arms.

Chapter Eight

They slipped under the iron railing and dropped down to the pebbly beach below, where they could be seen only by the sea gulls and pigeons that inhabited the area. Leaning against the rough cement siding of the causeway, Tip wrapped Kerry in his arms, pressing her head into his neck, and dropping random kisses on the top of her head while he squeezed her tight.

"Kerry, Kerry," he murmured. "Don't ever do that to me again. Promise me you'll never do that to me again."

"Do what to you?" She was inhaling deeply to capture as much of his scent as she could, sucking it up hungrily like a starving child. He smelled sweet and crisp, with an undertone of musky maleness, and she couldn't get enough of it to satisfy her senses.

"Never let me try and walk away from you again. That was the worst ten minutes of my entire life, walking away and thinking I had just blown everything."

Kerry giggled. "That wasn't ten minutes—it couldn't have been more than one minute at the most!"

"It felt like ten hours, and ten miles, too."

"I know what you mean." She had to pull away in order to give herself room to drop a soft lingering kiss on the warm spot where his collarbones met. Her lips sunk in gently and she sighed with relief. "I know exactly what you mean." She suddenly felt as if the entire afternoon had been the longest of her life, as well. "Oh, Tip, what are we going to do?"

"Do? Well, I don't know about you, but this feels fine for starters." He lifted a short lock of hair and planted a kiss on a very sensitive spot just behind Kerry's earlobe.

"I know...." she said with a sigh. "I know. But I mean about everything else."

"What else is there but this?" He continued kissing her while his hands stroked up and down her spine in a mesmerizing rhythm.

"Oh, God, there's everything else, and it's all such a mess!"

Tip pulled away reluctantly and searched her face for a long moment before replying. "I know, honey, I know. We've got a lot to talk about, and not all of it's pretty."

"What? Tell me what, Tip. I need to know."

He silenced her concerned questions with a finger across her lips. "Of course you need to know. And

you shall, I promise you. But first . . .'' he smiled his
slow, melting smile. ''First I think we both need
something else a lot more. At least, I know I do.''

And, taking her face in both hands, he pulled it toward his very slowly, so that his eyes could smile into
hers until the last possible moment before their lips
met in a tender embrace. Kerry made a soft, surren-
dering little sound of pleasure and collapsed against
his chest, her mouth opening, her neck arching upward to receive the full weight of his lips on hers. She
could feel his tongue, warm and delicate, darting between her parted teeth, and then his mouth probed
more deeply and he seemed to be drinking in her soul.

Together they slid down so that they were sitting,
leaning against the seawall, wrapped tightly in each
other's arms. Except for the unmistakable ocean tang
and the muffled sounds of activity coming from across
the bay, they might have been alone in a deserted room
in the middle of nowhere. In any case, it wouldn't have
mattered to Kerry if she had been sitting in the middle
of Copley Square at rush hour. She was so absorbed
in Tip's mouth and in the sensation of her mouth on
his that she would not have minded at all.

It was Kerry who slid her body back so that his
hands, which had been engaged in a gentle explora-
tion of her back, could slip around to just beneath her
breasts. He stopped a moment, then sighed at the
sensation of flesh through the thin material of her T-
shirt and began delicately massaging her nipples.
Kerry lifted her hands from around his waist and
slipped them around his neck, sliding her elbows all
the way up to allow him greater access to her breasts.
She felt no hesitation or shame about such abandon-

ment in a public place. All she wanted to do was to show Tip without words that she felt about him as he did about her.

His confession of love, granted in the heat of his anger had taken a while to sink in. Kerry had known at once what it meant to his career and to Tip personally to be giving up so much for her. But she was only beginning to realize what it might mean for her life as well. *Tip said he loved her!* He had also cursed the fact that he loved her, but he loved her just the same. A huge elation swelled up in Kerry so that she felt she might float up and away and out of his reach. She slid down lower into the gritty sand, pulling his body over hers as if his love might anchor her into reality.

Tip responded to her ardent gestures, growing more passionate as his kisses flowed like honey over her lips, down her chin and onto her breasts. Now, to have even the thin barrier of cloth between them seemed unbearable, and Kerry had to resist the urge to lift her shirt and release herself to the feel of his hard teeth against her bare nipples. She could feel Tip's arousal against her thigh as well, and knew that things were rapidly getting out of control. But she didn't much care.

This time it was Tip who felt the need to stop. "Wait a minute. Wait a minute," he said, pulling away from her and breathing hard. "I need this, but too much of a good thing is a bit dangerous around here, don't you think?"

Kerry looked up. She could see no one on the causeway but knew that all someone had to do was lean over the railing to see the two of them in their compromising position. She looked back at Tip and smiled. "My mind says yes, but my body says no."

"Our bodies seem to speak the same language," he replied huskily, drinking in the sight of her stretched beneath him. "But we'd better listen to our brains for the moment and avoid a possibly uncomfortable situation for our bodies later—like jail, for instance."

"I agree," she said, and reluctantly they pulled apart, straightened their clothing and gave themselves a moment to regain their composure.

"Now," Tip said, standing up and brushing off his suit, which seemed to have escaped the slightest wrinkle. "I suggest we get ourselves to a public place of less temptation and talk for a while." He smiled. "We can continue this later in a more private situation."

He helped Kerry to her feet, and they scrambled back up onto the causeway. A couple strolling a few yards behind them started at their sudden appearance over the railing, but Tip proceeded with total nonchalance, taking Kerry's arm and tucking it into his as they walked, making it seem as if there was nothing unusual in the world about a man in a three-piece suit appearing from beneath the seawall and strolling along with a disheveled woman in a T-shirt and jean shorts.

"Now," he said again, "where to begin?"

"Why don't you begin by telling me about that letter in your pocket?" she asked him. "I mean, I appreciate the gesture, but isn't it a little bit extreme?"

Tip waved his hand dismissively. "Forget about that. That's my decision and my problem. We've got something more important to discuss right now—that trial and what you're going to do about it."

Privately Kerry wondered how anything could be more important to Tip than his resignation from the attorney general's office, but she decided not to press him on it at the moment. "Why? What do I have to do about it? I thought I'd handled it pretty well, so far."

"You handled it better than pretty well, and you know it," he replied, squeezing her arm. "You handled it like a pro, and I was so proud of you . . . but that's not the problem. The problem is that once it gets out about your client knowing what Harvey and his pals were up to in that gazebo, things might not be so neat and easy anymore. For one thing, Harvey's pals will certainly sit up and take notice of your violinist. If Harvey figured out that Claudio had noticed him, it's only a matter of time before the others do, too. I meant what I said this morning about him being in some danger."

"You don't think they'd rather sacrifice Harvey than make the connections between them more obvious by doing something?"

"Who told you that?" he asked sharply.

"Tom did. He said that—"

"Damn." Tip scowled. "Pop's a good lawyer, but he sometimes lets his own integrity get in the way of his judgment." He looked away for a moment, then back to Kerry. "Tom's underestimating these fellows if he thinks they'll leave this alone, Kerry. What good will it do Santos and his friends to play dumb if Harvey decides to sing about them? I mean, it'll be good for us—for the A.G.'s office, that is—but it won't be so good for your client."

Kerry did not miss the fact that he was already trying to dissociate himself from the attorney general's office. "I know that," she said slowly. "And I think Tom knows it, too. I just think he might have felt that as long as Santos's people don't know what Claudio knows... That's why I didn't go to Wykoff with the information. That's why we didn't mention it this morning at the hearing."

"Of course. And you were smart not to." Tip stopped and looked away again, his lips pressed together in a thin line of concern. "I wish..." he murmured to himself.

Kerry, watching him, had a sudden realization. If she and her client didn't make it public knowledge that they knew about Harvey's underworld connections, then there was no reason to be afraid that Harvey's colleagues might find out. After all, Greg Harvey was in jail, and even if he wanted to get in touch with his colleagues, it was clear that they were steering away from any connection with him. There was a good chance that Harvey would be found guilty in the criminal court case, and the information would never have to be used. After all, the prosecution wouldn't have to explain *why* Claudio was shot to convict Harvey of shooting him. In that case, there was only one way that anyone could find out about it...unless, of course, they already knew.

"Tip." Kerry stopped walking. "Tip, does anybody else in your office know about Claudio's information? I mean, know that he knows..."

Tip stopped and faced her, taking a deep breath. "I don't know, Kerry. I just don't know. I didn't tell anyone. At least not in so many words, although I may have let on that I suspected as much before I found out for sure. But once I knew, and once I realized that you were going to get your indictment and a trial, I realized that there was a potential danger to Partero and to you. That's why I wrote that letter, because I knew I couldn't sit back and let that happen. If I had stayed, Kerry, I would have had to tell somebody what I knew, and then you can be sure that the information would have been leaked in the hope that it would prevent your client from pressing charges against Greg Harvey."

Kerry shook her head. "Do you mean to tell me," she asked, her voice soft with disbelief, "that the state attorney general's office would knowingly put an innocent man's life in danger simply to expedite their investigation of a known criminal?"

Tip let out his breath heavily. "I'd like to think that was an overstatement, Kerry, a gross exaggeration. I doubt, when it came right down to it, that the A.G. or anyone in his office would ever knowingly put anyone in danger, innocent or not. They must know, better than anyone, what's at stake, and I'm sure . . . yes, I'm sure they wouldn't have let things get that far out of hand." He spoke more for his own benefit than for Kerry's. "Of course I'm sure. I worked there, and I should know." But he didn't sound convinced.

"I don't believe it. I don't believe what you're implying, Tip."

He looked at her and smiled, reaching up to chuck her lightly under the chin. "That's what comes of working so closely with my father. You tend not to believe in the basic inability of mankind to deal with itself."

She stared at him. "I thought you weren't cynical."

Now he laughed, a little sadly. "You think I'm cynical? You should see the other guys! But seriously, Kerry, I don't think there's as much danger as that—as much danger as I may have led you or your client to believe. After all, it's like Tom told you: Santos and his people have nothing to gain by any connection with Greg Harvey and this shooting case, and Harvey has nothing to gain by connecting himself with them. So everybody will probably keep their mouths shut and Harvey's lawyers will plea bargain for the lightest sentence, and that will be the end of that. In any case, except for the civil case, which you'll probably win handily, your client is now just a witness for the state. And the state takes care of its witnesses, no matter how reluctantly."

Now it was Kerry's turn to stare away out to sea, her face averted from Tip's. Why was he scaring her with all this talk about danger? "Does that include Claudio keeping his mouth shut?" she asked quietly.

Tip took her by the shoulders and turned her around to face him. "Kerry, listen. That judge was absolutely right this morning in remanding the case over to the jury. We knew that, which is why we made no attempt to stop it. All the rest was just idle threat. And this talk about danger is pretty much the same thing. Just speculation. In all probability, Claudio will never have to mention what he knows about Greg Harvey and the others, and no one will ever find out he knows it, and everything will turn out all right. Want to know what I think will really happen? Harvey'll get a sentence for assault with a deadly weapon instead of attempted murder. You'll get your client a nice settlement, which will spend years in appeals court, and the A.G.'s office will eventually get Santos, which is what they really want in the first place. This whole mess will have turned out to be a tempest in a teapot."

"That's what you really think?" she asked, looking at him closely.

He smiled warmly. "That's what I really think."

"Then why all this scare talk, Tip? And why did you write that letter of resignation?"

The smile disappeared. "Let's just say I've learned my limits. You were the catalyst, Kerry, but this has been brewing in me for a long time. Believe me, a long, long time."

She nodded. "Now that," she said with a small smile of her own, "I believe."

He laughed. "Well, I'm glad I've managed to convince you of something this afternoon." He put his arm around her and nibbled briefly at the nape of her neck. "Now, what do you say we go back to my apartment and I can convince you of a few other important points? Like how I feel about you, and what I want to do with you, and . . ." His voice trailed off into a low sexy growl.

Kerry felt the resonance of his voice vibrating deeply through her body, but she leaned away. "I'd like to do that, Tip. I'd love to, more than anything. But . . ."

"But what?" He pulled away, real concern on his face.

She couldn't help laughing. "Now, don't take this personally . . ." she chided, and stroked his smooth cheek until she had produced a reluctant smile. "But I really have to think, Tip. About the case, I mean."

"What about? I've already told you . . ."

"I know what you told me, and I believe all of what you said. But that doesn't alter the main point. I have to think about my client, and what's best for my client. Claudio's been through hell, Tip, and it's my responsibility to see to it that he doesn't get put through any more. I have to think of his welfare even before I think about the merits of the case. If there's any danger, any chance of danger to him or his family—" She broke off and shook her head. "I have to think of him before I think about myself, too. You understand that, don't you?"

Tip nodded gravely. "I know what you mean. I just wish..." He sighed deeply. "I just wish I could make it all easier for you, that's all."

She smiled. "That's not what you're here for," she said tenderly. "Although I must admit it's a nice switch from your previous stand on the matter."

"I know. But I do want to help. As far as I can, of course, without betraying my... former allegiance."

Kerry understood what it cost him to refer to his job in the past tense, despite the fact that it was not yet official. She put her arms around him and hugged him warmly. "I know you want to help. And you've already done more than you know." She lifted her face away to look into his. "You've made me very happy this afternoon, believe it or not."

He kissed her with lingering hunger. "I want you to come home with me, to make love with me, Kerry."

"I know. I know. You just have to let... I have to think this thing through, first, Tip. I owe it to my client, and to myself. Please."

Tip released her slowly. "I understand. I just went through the same thing myself this morning after I left you at the courthouse. But promise me you'll come to me when you've decided what to do. We don't have to talk about it...." He grinned briefly but brilliantly. "As a matter of fact, I have every intention of not talking about anything at all, all night long, once I get you in my arms."

She could feel the heat of his gaze and nearly decided to forget about her scruples and to go home with him right away. But he leaned forward and kissed her swiftly, and then moved away. "I live at Harbor Towers," he told her. "In the East Tower, apartment twelve-oh-four." He paused, raking her once more with a longing look. "I'll be waiting there for you when, and if, you're ready to come to me."

Kerry shook her head. "Not if, Tip. There's no need for an if. I'll be there as soon as I can."

She stood and watched him stride away. The sun had dipped even lower and she had to shield her eyes as he got into his blue BMW and pulled away from the curb. She smiled to herself. Tip Sullivan loved the good things in life: good clothing, good cars, good food—and he loved her, which made her feel good about herself.

It did not, however, change the fact that she had to do some serious thinking about Claudio Partero and his case against Greg Harvey. She understood now that Tip had overstated his estimation of the possible dangers only in the hope of talking her out of handling the case—but he must have been really concerned on some level. After all, once the case was taken over by the state, Claudio would be nothing more than a witness for the prosecution, and Kerry's role, aside from handling the private civil suit for damages, would be purely advisory. But she felt responsible for Claudio, just as she knew that Tip felt responsible for her. And she had to think about Claudio's best interests before anything else.

She climbed up onto the railing and hooked her feet under the lower rail, feeling the setting sun warm her back as she stared out at the jumble of harbor activity before her. A lot of boats were coming into the harbour: fishing boats, tankers and scores of tiny pleasure boats, all vying for space in the narrow channel known as Hull Gut. Above them, jumbo jets dipped and soared, their roar muted to a dull rumble by the haze across the water. Kerry sighed and tried to focus on the subject at hand. What really was at stake here? Was it possible that in going through with the case, her client had gotten himself into even deeper trouble than he had been before getting shot? And had she, by encouraging him to go ahead with the case, been the instrument of his undoing? The very thought made her shudder, and she had to remind herself that there wasn't as much danger as Tip had tried to make her believe earlier. After all, even if it did leak out—and she certainly hoped it didn't—all Santos and his colleagues would have to do would be to deny any allegations that they were connected with Greg Harvey. There was certainly no hard evidence connecting them to the Partero shooting—Claudio's testimony would not hold up for a moment except where Harvey was concerned—and no judge or jury would take Greg Harvey's accusations as the truth.

She knew that, and she knew that everyone else knew it, including Greg Harvey and his friends. Otherwise Harvey would not be so scared and so alone.

But rational knowledge and intuition are two different things. And, at the moment, Kerry's nonrational processes had the upper hand. The only thing she was able to figure out, after nearly an hour alone leaning on the causeway railing, was that it probably wouldn't matter either way. Regardless of whether Claudio continued with the case, the information that he knew more than he seemed to know could leak out. So the only thing to do was to protect him as much as possible until it became clear that there would be no reprisals from Santos and his friends.

It wasn't really a decision as Kerry had pretty much already decided that the best thing to do would be nothing at all until the following day, when she could hold a powwow with Tom and Tip. It was good that Tip wasn't connected with the case anymore, since she could use his judgment and inside knowledge. But she could not help feeling badly that he believed he had to resign. Wouldn't it be possible for him to simply take himself off this one particular case? she wondered. She would have to talk to him about it—but not this evening, she amended. This evening they had other things on the agenda.

It was nearly dark when Kerry left the causeway and headed for the subway station. Cars were parked all the way around the crescent that bordered the beach, but there was no one in sight. An abandoned beach house, still smelling slightly of salt and damp, stood empty a short distance away, its windows vacant and forbidding. Kerry knew that teenaged kids often hung out within its cool confines during the day, smoking cigarettes and haranguing passersby. It did not look inhabited this evening, but just to be safe, she crossed over to the other side, to the narrow strip of tall bushes that separated the beach from the row houses on the far side of the crescent.

She was just about to cross back over when someone grabbed her arm roughly from behind and pulled her back into the thick shrubs. She was about to cry out, but a thick hand clamped down over her mouth, crushing her lip against her teeth until she could taste a trickle of blood.

Her first reaction was anger, and she kicked back with her sandaled foot as hard as she could. But her foot came in contact with nothing but air, and it flashed through her mind that she was in real danger.

Then the fear overtook her, paralyzing both her body and her voice, so that she went suddenly still and limp in her assailant's arms. She tried to force her mind to think clearly, but it refused. She could not even form a mental picture of her assailant except to know that he was big and strong and knew what he was doing.

"Come on over here, little lady," said another voice, farther behind her and off to one side. "We just wanna talk to you is all. Careful Bobby. Don't hurt her now."

But Bobby did not relax his grip around Kerry's shoulder and chest as he walked her quickly over to a waiting car. Kerry was sure that she would be seen as they crossed the sidewalk and stepped off the curb, but if anyone saw them, she knew, they would probably have the good sense not to interfere. She could only hope that a concerned resident might see her being kidnapped and report the license number to the police. She herself could not see the car well enough to identify its make, let alone its license number. All she could do was concentrate on putting one foot in front of the other and on continuing to breathe despite the sharp, stabbing pain of fear that accompanied each breath.

"Okay, right in here now, that's right. Just slide in there and you'll be just fine," the man behind her instructed her in a voice that sounded soft, almost fatherly, in contrast to his rough handling. Kerry ducked her head inside the rear door and slid along the leather seat. The man named Bobby slid in after her, holding her arm pinned behind her so that she could not turn around and see his face.

A second later the other rear door opened and a short, balding man in a light-colored suit and dark glasses entered. Involuntarily she gasped. She had not expected an older man, having unconsciously connected her earlier fear about the teenagers in the beach house with her abduction. Now she could only pray that some of those teenagers had seen her being pulled away.

She looked forward and saw that there was no one in the driver's seat. "What are you going to do to me?" she asked. Her voice came out in a tiny squeal, and she sounded hopelessly inadequate to deal with the situation. She bit back tears. She refused to give in to tears. She somehow felt that tears would seal her unknown fate. "Where are you taking me?"

The balding man gestured at the front seat with a little smile. "Now, how could we be taking you anywhere without a driver? You're not thinking, Miss Sullivan. You're just not thinking."

Kerry nodded stupidly and tried to get her brain to function so that she could figure out what her options were. Certainly escape was out of the question, since her exits were both guarded by men larger than she. Other than that, nothing she could think of sounded very good at all.

It took her a full minute to realize what the man had said. "You said my name!" she cried, startled out of her fear for a moment. "How did you know my name?"

"Aw, Miss Sullivan, we know a lot about you. You got to give us credit for being smart at least."

She closed her eyes and swallowed hard, tasting blood. So this was not a random, isolated abduction. These men were here for a purpose, and it was beginning to dawn on her shocked brain what that purpose might be. "Who are you?" she demanded in a stronger voice. "What's your name?"

"Hey, lady lawyer, I said we were smart. It'd be pretty stupid of me to tell you my name, now wouldn't it?"

"I had a friend with me," Kerry retorted, trying to sound menacing. "I had a friend with me, and I'm sure he saw you and has gone to get the police. So you'd better—"

"Shut up!" It was Bobby's voice, behind her, and it didn't sound pleasant at all anymore. Still, the bald man was smiling with frightening geniality.

"There was no one with you, Miss Sullivan, so don't even bother. Besides, you've got nothing to worry about. What do you think we're gonna do to you, huh?"

Kerry did not answer, but lifted her fingers and pressed them gingerly against her lip where she had bitten it. It felt swollen, but there was no blood on her finger when she pulled it away.

"Now, now, you think we're gonna rape you? You think we want to hurt a pretty little lady like you?" Baldie reached out and touched her lip tenderly. She yanked her face away as if he had burned her. Baldie chuckled.

"No, we just wanna talk to you is all, like I said. We just wanna ask you a few questions about your friend Claudio. You know, the fiddle player with the hole in his shoulder?"

Even though Kerry had suspected that this was the reason for her attack, the mention of Claudio's name made her freeze with fear. So this was it. Everything she had been afraid but unwilling to believe might happen was happening. And to her.

"I don't know what you're talking about," she stammered.

"Of course you do. He's your client, remember? The one you got an indictment for, against one Mr. Greg Harvey?"

"Are you an associate of Mr. Harvey's?"

Baldie laughed menacingly. "Now I'd be a real fool to answer that question, wouldn't I? You must think we're all fools, Miss Sullivan, to go around getting your client messed up with something he doesn't understand. You must think we're really dumb to let you get away with a thing like that."

"My client was shot," Kerry said, trying to keep the hysteria out of her voice so she could think straight. "And we intend to see that justice is done."

The man pursed his thick lips thoughtfully. "Sounds good to me," he remarked. "Only thing is, we heard that your client has this mistaken idea that Mr. Harvey might be connected with some...well, let's just say some people who don't want to be connected with Mr. Harvey. And that your client might feel he needs to tell this information—false as it is, of course—to the judge." His hand came up and brushed against Kerry's lips again, but this time Bobby had taken her head in his hands so that she could not pull away. "And you know, Miss Sullivan, our friends don't want any judge to get the wrong impression about them. They don't want that at all."

"Get your hands off me," Kerry grated out. She could feel the hairs rising on the back of her neck and she was vaguely nauseous.

He didn't stop. "Anyway, the thing is, we want to impress upon your client—and you, of course—that it would be stupid of him to discuss any possible activities he may think he saw around the gazebo lately. Stupid, because if he does, then the jury will have a hard time believing that that shooting was only a personal affair. And you see, Miss Sullivan, if they think it's more than that, then they might make a connection we don't want, and we'll have to assume that Mr. Partero knows more than he says he does. And we wouldn't want that, now would we?"

"What if Greg Harvey talks?" she asked, resisting the temptation to spit on his fingers as she spoke. "Then your friends will really be in trouble, won't they?"

She could not see Baldie's eyes behind his dark glasses, but she could see his mouth harden into a tight, angry line. "Listen, kiddo, you worry about your people and we'll worry about ours. I'm telling you to see to it that your fiddle player doesn't make too much loud music. Because if he does, he's not gonna be happy with the results." He looked over her head at Bobby. "Get her outta here. And tell our friends that we're ready to go."

Bobby opened the door on his side and pulled Kerry out behind him. Twisting her arm into the same position as before, he walked across the street with her. To any passersby, they would look as if they were arm in arm. He stopped when they reached the opposite sidewalk, just ahead of the beach house.

"Now, you just start walking to wherever you were going," he instructed her. "Just keep walking and don't look back. You understand?"

Kerry nodded dumbly, waiting for him to let go of her arm. As soon as he did, she turned and walked rapidly in the direction of the subway station, resisting the urge to run since she knew that would only accelerate her panic. She could feel his eyes behind her as he waited and watched on the sidewalk. Then she heard his steps moving in the opposite direction.

She walked a few steps farther before she gave in to the irresistible impulse to turn around. As she did, she caught a glimpse of a car in the alleyway alongside the beach house. She could not tell if it was the same car she had been in or not, but she thought not since the street was divided by a concrete median and she hadn't heard a car start up. As she looked, mesmerized despite her terror, the rear lights of the car went on and it began to pull out. It was a long black sedan, maybe a Cadillac, maybe even a limousine. But she could not see the license plate. What she did see was one of the rear doors open. By the interior light and the lurid red glow of the taillights, she saw three or four men inside. One of them, the one sitting closest to her, looked vaguely familiar. Something about his patrician profile and prominent nose...but Kerry was in no condition to stick around and figure it out. She turned on her heel and ran.

Chapter Nine

Afterward, Kerry couldn't remember how she had gotten herself to Tip's apartment—shock and terror had quickly taken their toll, so that she could only respond automatically to her needs. And she had needed Tip badly.

She assumed she had taken the subway, although Tip was sure he had looked out his street-side window and seen a cab screeching to a halt outside his building shortly before Kerry arrived, breathless and shaking at his front door. When she looked in her wallet she found that almost all her money was gone but she insisted to Tip that she never indulged in cabs, even in crisis situations.

"Besides," she pointed out, fixating on the irrelevant details of her flight in order to avoid the more horrible memories of her ordeal, "that guy Bobby, the one who pinned me from behind? He might have taken the money. I'm sure I had a twenty at least, and now it's gone."

Tip was pouring a shot of very good brandy down her throat, holding her head against his shoulder and cradling her as if she were an infant. "Those guys don't bother rifling through wallets, Kerry, believe me." His voice was tight with rage and frustration. "I'm sure you had the good sense to take a cab, even though you don't remember it now. After all, you've had a terrible shock." His fingers tightened around the stem of the brandy snifter until it looked like it might break. "Damn!" he swore explosively. "If only I hadn't left you there! I should have insisted that you come home with me. I should have known there would be trouble!"

"How could you possibly have known?" The brandy was doing its work and Kerry's shivering was slowing down. "Besides," she added, "I wouldn't have listened to you anyway." She turned and looked out the huge picture window that faced the tan tweed sofa on which they sat. The drapes were still open and the view to the south revealed the vast panorama of Boston Harbor. To the right, she could see the twinkling lights of the downtown skyscrapers against the now dark night sky. To the left, across the harbor, were the blue lights of the Logan Airport runaway. And straight ahead, only a mile or two directly south, was Carson Beach.... The shuddering began again with a vengeance.

"Hey, hey, slow down! Relax. It's all right now. You're safe here." Tip wrapped her more tightly in his arms, as if he could absorb her fear through his body.

Kerry tried to let her body go limp against his warm bulk.

"I know, I know," she whispered through chattering teeth. "I just can't seem to stop..."

"Shhh. It's okay, sweetie. Why don't you just let it all out in tears? That'll make you feel better, I'm sure."

Kerry shook her head. "I can't," she explained. "I can't cry about it. I don't know... I'm too confused, too angry for that I guess. I just wish I could... stop this shaking."

"Here." Tip grabbed his jacket from the back of a nearby chair. "Snuggle up into this while I go and make some hot tea. Hot tea and brandy, that oughta do the trick."

He got up and Kerry managed a weak, grateful smile. "That something you learned from old Tom?" she asked.

He turned and flashed her his beautiful grin. "Nope. Something I learned from old Mary, my mother. But she used to use it on Dad—after he'd been out all night in the cold, 'on a job,' as he used to tell her." He cocked his head. "I really don't think it ever occurred to my mother that Tom probably inhaled more alcohol in one working night that she did in a month of Sundays." He moved into the small kitchen off the dining area, and Kerry could hear him pouring water into a kettle. "I don't think it mattered much to her either, come to think of it."

Kerry did not reply but pulled her legs up underneath Tip's jacket and rested her elbows on her knees. She looked around at the large one bedroom unit. She had never been inside one of the Harbor Towers apartments before, but she had heard a lot about their spectacular views. Everything she had heard was right, but she hadn't expected Tip's place to be so nice on the inside as well. The walls were painted pale beige except for the wall behind the sofa, which was a deep saddle-brown semigloss that glowed like leather in the warm light of a tiffany lamp. The furniture was very masculine looking, but not excessively so. Besides the tweed couch, there was a modern-looking leather recliner in a pretty shade of dark blue and a circular Oriental on the floor that picked up the color and added accents of deep scarlet. A matching set of side chairs in a muted print sat on either side of an inactive small wood-burning stove that was pretty enough to double as a sculpture, with its clean black lines and row of blue delft tiles. There were several good prints on the walls.

It was the apartment of a man who had risen above his humble origins without straining to get there. Tip's tastes were acquired but backed by a solid sense of himself and of quality. He could easily have been born into rooms like this, she found herself thinking, and thought also of Tom's big dilapidated house on Dorchester. The furniture there was strictly showroom stuff, and she was sure that no one had given any of it a second thought since Mary Sullivan's death years before. Kerry wasn't sure if she liked the contrast between Tom's home and his son's or if she was saddened by it. But it certainly wasn't any time to dwell on the subject.

Tip returned with a mug of steaming tea and set it down on the coffee table. He picked up the brandy bottle and poured a stiff dose of it into the mug before handing it to Kerry.

"Here. Careful, it's very hot. That's good, sip slowly. There. Feeling any better?"

Kerry could feel the alcoholic steam rising up into her nostrils and seeping into her brain. The shivering had stopped again, and she managed a more certain smile. "Feeling a lot better. Your mother knew what she was doing."

"You bet she did." Tip sat down and pulled the jacket closer around her shoulders. "Now," he said gently, "you feel up to starting from the beginning, or you want to wait a bit more?"

Kerry looked at him with frightened eyes.

"We have to talk about it," he said tenderly. "I can't let you forget the details of this Kerry, much as I wish you could. And you know you won't really forget. Better to get it all out now."

Kerry took another swallow of tea, sighed and nodded. "You're right, of course. And I'm all right. I'm ready now." She put the tea down and settled back, pulling herself into a tighter ball on the couch.

"We can wait if you're not up to it," Tip reminded her. His eyes were warm, but his face was drawn with concern, and Kerry could see his pulse throbbing inside the open collar of his button-down shirt.

"Hey," she said, smiling as she reached out her hand from beneath the jacket and touched his arm. "I'm all right, really I am. Thanks for being so worried, but I'm okay."

Tip didn't look all that convinced, but he nodded, taking her hand and tucking it tightly against his chest. Kerry snuggled closer and began to talk. She told him with as much lawyerly detail as she could muster, exactly what had happened and in what sequence. She tried to recall verbatim the conversation she had had with Baldie, and when she couldn't, she mentioned that the words were her own and not exact. She was as graphic as possible about the physical assault—how she had been grabbed, where on her body and how hard she had been held—despite the fact that she saw Tip's face get red then white with barely repressed fury as she spoke.

And she did not leave out what she had seen as she was leaving the scene of the crime—the big car, parked alongside the abandoned beach house, and the four profiles she had seen within. Although she did not forget that this was the second time in a week that she had had to relate a harrowing and traumatic tale, she seemed to gain control and confidence as she spoke. By the time she had finished her narrative, the combination of the brandied tea and her own strong voice made her feel more relaxed.

Tip sat very still and looked at her for a few moments. Then he stood up and began pacing in front of the couch, every muscle in his body betraying his agitation. "Okay, Okay," he muttered, more to himself than to her. "so now we know where we stand with these guys. Now everything is on the table. They want you and Claudio to go ahead, but they don't want him to talk about why he thinks Greg Harvey might have taken a shot at him. And of course, that throws your motive right out the window. The state's case is shot. The most he can hope for will be an assault with a dangerous weapon conviction. And when you go to prosecute your civil award case, that's sure to work against you." He was moving quickly, with panther grace, turning sharply when he reached either end of the couch. Kerry's eyes hurt from watching him move above her.

"So, what do you think we ought to do about it?" she asked.

"Do?" He stopped as if surprised to see her sitting there. "Well, call the police, of course. That's the first order of business. Call the police." He looked as if he had just come to that conclusion himself, and moved to the phone that sat between the two chintz chairs.

"No, Tip, wait!"

"Wait?" He stopped with the receiver in his hands. "Why wait?"

"Because," she said, not knowing quite why. "Because I'm not quite ready to go through that whole rigamarole again just yet. Because I want to think it through for myself to see where we stand." She took a deep breath. "And because I'm scared."

He was back at the couch in an instant, stroking her hair away from her pale face. "I know you are, honey. And that's why we should call the police. This thing has gone far enough. Let me call Wykoff and get him over here. That way you can tell him at your own pace and we can decide how to handle it together."

Kerry shook her head slowly. "What I don't understand is how they knew about it. How did they know that Claudio knew about Santos and the others? Did they get to Harvey? And if they did, why would he bother to tell them, since it would only mean his position with them was in greater jeopardy?"

They looked at each other. "And if he didn't tell them," Tip said, finishing Kerry's thought for her, "who did?"

They were silent for a moment, staring into each other's eyes. Suddenly Kerry shuddered again. "That man's voice," she said. "That nice, fatherly voice! I couldn't believe he was threatening me with that kindly voice."

Tip smiled thinly. "Welcome to the lovely world of high crime, Miss Sullivan, where a man who looks nice enough to be your own grandpa can threaten your life without missing a beat."

"Yeah." An image of Baldie flashed violently through her mind followed by mental picture of the long limousine parked alongside the beach house. Kerry hadn't been close enough to recognize anyone in that car. Why then, did the image keep recurring to her? Something about it stuck in her craw and stirred her intuition. She just didn't know what it was.

"Don't call Wykoff just yet, Tip," she reiterated. "First I have to decide what I'm going to do. What Claudio should do, I mean." She looked up at Tip, her eyes big with the question. "Tip, do you think I should convince him to drop out of the case? I mean, if he doesn't testify, the government doesn't have a case against Harvey at all, and the whole thing will have to be dropped."

"That's true. But the prosecutors could make it pretty difficult for Claudio to refuse to testify. They could hold him in contempt, even serve a warrant for his arrest if he doesn't cooperate. After all, it's their case now, and he's just a witness for the prosecution."

"I know." Kerry realized that her brain was still not functioning properly, or she would have remembered that basic fact herself. "It's ironic, isn't it? I was so gung ho, pushing for Claudio to get the case remanded to the jury, and now, when I want him out of it, I can't."

"Are you sure you want him out of it?" Tip asked carefully.

Kerry was surprised. "Well, I suppose... I mean, after what happened tonight, I just figured that it would be safer for everyone involved if the whole thing stopped here."

Tip shook his head slightly. "I'm afraid it's even further out of our hands than that, Ker. It couldn't stop here even if we wanted it to. That's the miserable thing about it all."

Kerry knew that Tip was right. She knew that even if Claudio did not testify, which would never happen, his silence would be as much an admission of knowledge as his speech. Baldie's warning did no good at all—the damage was already done. She drew in her breath raggedly and tried to let it out in a smooth, relaxing stream, but it kept on getting caught in her chest, and she coughed.

Tip leaned over to pat her on the back, and Kerry spoke with her head bent over her bare thighs, staring at the faint tan line where her legs disappeared into her shorts. "You still think we have to go through with it, don't you, Tip?" Tip did not reply. "That's why you want me to call Wykoff. You want to get police protection for Claudio, don't you?"

"And you, too, if necessary," was all he would say. His voice was grave and subdued.

Kerry had stopped coughing, but when she raised her head, her eyes were full of tears. Tip saw them and immediately softened. "Oh, honey," he murmured, gathering her into his arms. "I don't want to scare you more than you're already scared. God knows, that's the last thing I'd ever want to do." He groaned softly. "I think you should do whatever makes you feel safest. We can get Tom to handle the case from now on. Get you totally out of it. Maybe you can even go away for a while, visit friends or something. We'll take care of Claudio, and you'll have nothing to worry about. I promise you, I'll do whatever I can...." His words disappeared as he hugged her more tightly against him, his hands cradling her head against his neck.

When Kerry looked up her face was still tear-stained, but she knew what she wanted to do.

"Tip," she whispered, "I've had enough of all this for now."

"I know, I know. What do you want? Whatever you want..."

Kerry stared at him, her eyes searching his, full of need and desire. "I want you to make love to me, Tip," she whispered urgently. "I want you to make love to me right here, right now. Help me forget, for just a little while."

She did not move to kiss him, feeling that her request might put him off, even strike him as disgusting. But she was in no mood to go against her impulses, and at that moment the strongest impulse she had was to lose herself in the ardent power of Tip's lovemaking.

He looked back at her for a long moment, examining her features as if trying to assess the extent of her need and the exact quality of her mood. Whatever he found there obviously made up his mind for him, because with a deep sigh he gathered her against him, crushing her mouth with his.

This was no time for gentle tenderness. Kerry responded to that first touch as if a live wire had been ignited deep inside her. She sprang against him, wrapping her arms around his neck as if she needed to hold on to Tip or drown. Her lips replied to his with hungry urgency, clinging hard and probing deep, seeking solace in the overwhelming rush of desire that surfaced. If she had had time to think about it, Kerry might have been appalled by her body's response. Here she was, fresh from yet another trauma, and once again, all she wanted was Tip's body covering hers with erotic pleasure. The first time it had happened it had seemed an aberration. Now it seemed as if some perverse pattern was emerging, some unhealthy reaction to stress that triggered this great physical need.

But it had never happened to her before she met him, and the need was very specific—it was Tip she wanted, not just anybody. He answered a call in her, filled the spaces that fear opened deep inside her heart. By making love to him, Kerry was reassuring herself that she was alive and well, and that the positive things in life, like love and sex and two people belonging together, still existed in a world that seemed to be teetering at the edge of madness.

In any case, Kerry was in no position to be analyzing her reaction. She was far too involved in Tip's mouth, and in the hands that swept up and down the sides of her ribs, setting the skin beneath her T-shirt quivering with desire. His fingertips brushed the edges of her breasts, stirring them until the nipples blossomed like flowers against the thin material.

They were sitting next to each other on the couch, but the power of their embrace carried them forward and on to their knees on the thick rug. In this position their torsos were free to meet, and they pressed together until Kerry thought there was no air left in her lungs to breathe. But his kisses provided her with oxygen and that something she needed much more—the power of his desire for her. In order to magnify the sensations, Kerry lifted her arms and Tip responded instantly by pulling her shirt over her head. Without giving a moment's thought to what he was doing, he ripped the buttons of his own shirt open, exposing the bronze muscles of his chest to her soft and eager breasts. Kerry nearly cried out at that first touch of skin against skin—her nipples were so sensitive that the pleasure was very near to pain.

Then, when Tip bent his head and moved his lips down her throat toward her breasts, she did cry out. He looked up quickly, his face full of passion and concern.

"No," she whispered hoarsely. "I don't mean stop. Please don't stop." She thrust her fingers into his thick hair and cradled his head as he bent back to her throat. He made his way with lingering deliberation until he could bend no lower without crouching. Then, wrapping his arms more tightly around her ribs, he actually picked her up so that his mouth was level with her breasts. Kerry felt weightless and immovable in his arms, and pressed herself more closely against his hips as if she would take root there.

Tip applied his lips and tongue and teeth to her nipples, first one and then the other, in ever-tightening circles of sensation that felt like a noose of pleasure closing around Kerry's skin. By the time he had zeroed in on the epicenter of sensation, Kerry's head was thrown back in abandonment to gratification. Then, using one hand and without taking his mouth from her breast, he undid the snap and zipper on her shorts and slipped them down to her knees along with her cotton bikini underwear.

Kerry lifted her body, carefully moving her legs to get free of the scanty clothing without sacrificing one iota of attention to what was happening higher up. Now her legs were free to wrap around Tip's waist, and her arms dipped down his back to slip inside the waistband of his slacks and caress the hard mounds of his buttocks. She pressed her mouth to the top of his head, reveling in her nudity and abandonment. Kerry could feel the heat of her loins rubbing against Tip's waist, and the friction of bare flesh against cloth only heightened the excitement.

Now Tip set her down and, again using his strength, lifted her torso so that his mouth could reach even lower. He was still kneeling, but Kerry was raised halfway to her feet, although they could not have supported her had she tried to stand. His lips flowed like a river of hot lava across the taut and tingling flesh of her belly, darting in and out of her belly button and over the prominent bones of her hips. Kerry moved forward gently to accommodate him. She felt like a flower growing out of the fertile pleasure of his mouth, bursting into rich blossom at his touch.

Then his lips traveled farther still, moving across the mound of her loins and into the soft dark hair between her legs. Now Kerry could not support herself and crumpled against him, her hands and mouth seeking to give back what had been given in such great measure. They fell together on the rug, and Tip slipped out of his pants as best he could while the frenzy of Kerry's lips covered him. She drank in the smooth skin of his chest and delved into the sharp ripples of his rib cage. Her hands moved rhythmically up and down his legs, reveling in the rough hair that covered his thighs and grew denser yet softer as her fingers traveled upward. At his hips, her hands and mouth met in their explorations.

Suddenly she felt herself being lifted again, and she turned her body so that she was hovering over Tip as he lay on his back. He positioned her carefully astride his hips and lowered her gently. Kerry thought she would melt as the first wave of heat shot up through her hips like a leaping stag afire. She arched her back and threw back her head and let out a moan that seemed to release the last vestiges of tension. Then she was free to concentrate on the slow rocking rhythm of their coupling. She bent her head so that their eyes locked together as they loved. She saw the flames reflected in Tip's hot gaze, felt the heat from his parted lips. Her deep and ragged breath flowed over him like a rising river, reaching higher up on the shore of sensation with each thrust and parry.

His hands were tangled in the tousled mop of her hair, his fingers cupping her face. She braced her arms on either side of his shoulders and tried to increase the rhythm without losing control of the tight rein of her desire. But she was not able to maintain control for long. With a sudden fierce onslaught, she reached her peak and arched her body back, crying out in ecstasy as wave after wave of hot passion overcame her.

But it was not over yet. Before she could recover Tip had gently pulled her down along his damp torso and rolled them over so that he now rode above her. While Kerry's vision was still clearing from the first wave, he began building slowly but resoundingly to the second. Kerry felt one brief piercing shock of panic—she thought she might lose control altogether if she reached that height again so quickly. But she had no choice. She could only cling to Tip and abandon herself to the ocean of heat and light that now bore down on them both like a tidal wave. Fears, doubts, all were forgotten in the certainty of satiation and in the comfort of knowing that she was loved as she loved.

"I do love you, Tip," she said softly a very long time afterward.

Tip's throaty chuckle seemed to rise from deep in the pit of his stomach. "Well I'm glad to hear that," he said, turning over on his side. "I was beginning to think you were just using me for emotional obliteration."

Kerry sat up suddenly. "Oh, no, not that! I don't want you to ever think that!"

"Easy, girl, easy. Lie back down and stop panicking." He pressed his warm hand against the declivity between her breasts and pushed her gently back into a prone position.

"It's not like that, though, Tip," she told him earnestly. "I know it may seem strange, the way we end up making love after I've been through these traumatic experiences, but it has nothing to do with them. I mean, it does, but it doesn't mean that . . ."

"Hush, now, will you?" He placed one hand over her mouth and then replaced it tenderly with his lips. "Kerry Sullivan, you don't have to put yourself through this, you know. I'm not stupid, after all." He smiled slowly. "I know when I'm being loved."

She reached up and traced the outlines of the smile. "As long as you know," she murmured.

"I know. And so should you. So you can just forget your little guilt trip and rest assured. We both know what's happening here; it's just surprising that it didn't happen sooner, considering the way our lives are connected."

"Sort of like kismet, isn't it?"

He nodded. "And the fact that our lives happen to be going crazy at the moment doesn't mean that's the only reason we need each other, believe me."

Kerry bit her lip. "You know, I almost forgot. You wrote a letter of resignation, didn't you? Because of me, your career is in jeopardy. Tip . . ."

"Don't 'Tip' me," he retorted, making an effort to appear stern. "That's the last thing on my mind right now."

"What's first? The trial? Baldie and those guys at Carson beach?"

He appeared to be considering the answer for a moment or two, and then suddenly he scooped her up in his arms again. "That's two guesses wrong," he said, tickling her ear with his breath as he dropped soft little kisses along the side of her neck. "You get one more try."

"And so do you," she giggled as their lips and bodies met yet again.

By the next morning, however, both Tip and Kerry were ready to tackle the business end of their predicament. Kerry knew that he had been right in warning her that she now had little choice in the matter of Greg Harvey's trial. Even if she were able to convince Claudio not to testify after all the effort they had made, she would only be getting him into deeper trouble than he was already in. Either way, the fact that he knew more about Greg Harvey's connections than he had admitted so far was already working against him. Things had already gotten out of control.

Tip and Kerry decided that their only possible course of action was to go directly to the police and let Detective Wykoff know how things stood. Although he would probably be angry that he hadn't been told everything about Claudio's testimony right from the start, he could at least arrange for some protection for Claudio while the trial was going on. Tip's first fear was that Santos's men would try to convince Claudio the same way they had tried to convince Kerry—and that they wouldn't be as gentle with him as they had been with her. Remembering all too clearly what their definition of gentle had been like, Kerry was only too eager to agree.

Tip also felt that Greg Harvey might be in need of protection. He still wasn't sure how the information about Claudio's knowledge had leaked, but if it hadn't been Greg Harvey who told Santos and his men, then Harvey himself might be in some danger. Although

Kerry didn't see this as clearly as she saw the danger to Claudio, she agreed that it might be a wise move to see to it that as many people as possible were watched.

The strangest thing was that she felt little fear for herself. The previous night had been a nightmare, but somehow, in the strong light of day, it seemed unlikely that it could happen again. Her feeling wasn't based so much on intuition as it was on a sense of security. After all, she had been through the worst thing she could imagine, and she had survived. She now knew what she was up against, and that helped a lot. It helped too, to know that Tip was on her team and at her side. As long as she had him in her sight, she could not imagine plunging once again into the nightmare. And she had no intention of letting him out of her sight.

Tip called Tom and let him know what was happening, but he did not mention the attack on Kerry, knowing that his father would only worry helplessly on her account. Then he and Kerry went down to the station and asked to see Detective Wykoff.

They were kept waiting for nearly thirty minutes in the detective's grubby cubicle. Outside the glass partition they could hear the sounds of police business all around them. There was a lot of shouting and running around at one point, and Kerry felt her heartbeat accelerate. But Tip, seeing her look up apprehensively, squeezed her hand.

"It's okay," he reassured her. "Probably just the snack truck out in the corridor."

Kerry smiled. "You seem to be making a habit out of comforting me," she told him, her eyes shining with shy gratitude.

Tip did not return her smile. "And I intend to keep on doing it for a very long time," he told her gravely.

They were lost in each other's eyes when Wykoff stepped into the room. "And what do you two love-birds want?" he asked shortly.

Kerry turned around with a smile that melted instantly when she saw Wykoff's face. He looked drawn and haggard, as if he hadn't slept in days. And he looked angry, his small dark eyes burning out of his puffy face.

"What's wrong?" Tip asked him.

Wykoff waved the question aside and sat down heavily. "Police business. What's your problem, Sullivan?" He grinned wanly from Tip to Kerry. "Or should I say, Sullivan and Sullivan?"

Tip came right to the point. "Kerry was assaulted last night by some of Santos's men. They're trying to force her into getting her client to keep his mouth shut when the A.G.'s office calls him on the witness stand."

Wykoff turned to Kerry. "That true, Miss Sullivan?" Kerry nodded and gave him a brief explanation of what had happened, watching his jaw tighten as he listened. When she was done he turned back to Tip. "And what's your stake in this, Tip? You here as a representative of the A.G.'s office or what?"

Tip smiled thinly. "Hardly. I'm off the case. But we thought we should get to you and try and arrange some protection for Mr. Partero in case these fellows decide to keep on playing bully. You know, of course, that Partero knew more about Harvey's business connections than he admitted to you at first."

Wykoff looked at Kerry, pressed his lips together, and nodded curtly. "We do now," he said tersely.

Tip ignored his expression and went on. "We'll need protection for Greg Harvey, too."

"Why Harvey?" Wykoff shot the question at him.

"It's obvious, Stan. If Santos's men don't think they can get Partero to stop talking, they can certainly try to get Harvey to shut up. I know he's locked up in the Charles Street jail, but you and I both know that's hardly an impregnable fortress. And if someone really wanted to do some convincing, a prison visit could be pretty effective. Harvey's got nowhere to run."

"You're right," Wykoff said, leaning back heavily in the squeaky chair. "Right, but too late."

Kerry sat forward, suddenly rigid. "What is it? What's happened to Claudio?"

Wykoff shook his head disgustedly. "Nothing's happened to the star witness. You can bet that once the attorney general's office has him they're going to see to it that he stays had. Am I right, Tip?"

Tip had paled. "It's Harvey, isn't it?"

Wykoff didn't even bother to nod.

"What's Harvey?" Kerry looked from one man to the other. "Tell me what's happened to Harvey?"

"We found Harvey in his cell this morning," Wykoff said, lighting a cigarette. "He's dead."

Chapter Ten

Much to her own surprise, Kerry took this newest shock quite well. While Tip cursed under his breath and slumped back in his chair, Kerry leaned forward in hers and peppered Detective Wykoff with urgent questions. How had Greg Harvey died? When had it happened? Had anyone been to visit him or had anything suspicious happened earlier in the day?

Placing the fingertips of his hands together and examining them closely, Wykoff answered her patiently. "He was discovered early this morning by one of the guards who says he was definitely alive last night at lights-out. Charles Street is not a high-security facility, so there's no bed check, but the guard says he definitely talked to him about 9 P.M."

"How did he seem? Did the guard say how he seemed?"

Detective Wykoff smiled thinly. "Miss Sullivan, have you ever been locked up in the Charles Street jail? I suspect not, but you can imagine that no one in there is particularly upbeat." The smile disappeared. "The guard says he didn't notice anything unusual about the man, but then the guard might not have noticed if Harvey was blue in the face—sorry, that wasn't intended to be disrespectful. But the guards are not always as observant as they might be."

Kerry nodded, trying to form a mental picture in her mind. She had been to the jail once or twice to interview clients and had found it appropriately dismal but had never been beyond the public areas into the tall rows of cells. Most prisoners were taken to one of the larger facilities out of the city if they were going to be incarcerated for any length of time. "It's odd that Harvey was still at Charles Street, isn't it?" she asked. "I mean, he still had two or three weeks to go until trial."

"All our prisons are overcrowded. And Harvey's lawyers were still trying to get bail for him." He shook his head. "Obviously they were going to the wrong people."

"What about visitors? Did he have any visitors?"

"He had two visitors yesterday afternoon. One was his mother and the other a guy who gave what we believe to be a false name. He identified himself as Mr. Richard Harrington. No such name is registered to the address he gave, although we didn't find that out until this morning, of course."

Tip spoke for the first time. "You get a description of the guy?"

"Hell, we got a description of his mother, Sullivan. The guy was short, about fifty-five or sixty, well dressed, a little overweight. Bald, too."

Kerry took a deep breath and looked at Tip. "That's the man," she said. "The man who talked to me in the car last evening."

Wykoff did not seem surprised. "Any further identifying marks you can supply us with?"

Kerry thought. "Thick lips, and he was wearing dark glasses, so I couldn't see his eyes. But he had a big gold band on his finger. He looked..." She paused and then finished sheepishly. "He looked like he could be somebody's grandfather."

She saw Wykoff and Tip exchange glances over her head. "He could be," Wykoff remarked.

"Oh, and he had a nice voice, too. I mean, a voice that didn't sound like it belonged with what he was saying." She turned to Wykoff. "Does that man sound familiar to you, Detective?"

Wykoff pursed his lips. "Could be. He sure sounds like Harvey's visitor. We're talking to the mother now, since she came in after this other fellow. She says she didn't notice anything wrong with her son, except that he was asking her to get him bail money wherever she could." He snorted. "But Mama Harvey's a drinker, so I don't think anything makes much of an impression on her anymore."

"Poor Greg Harvey," Kerry murmured. She knew that Harvey was as much a victim as Claudio was and shuddered as she imagined what his fear must have felt like. Fear strong enough to make him take his own life. "How did he die, Detective Wykoff?"

"He took a massive overdose of Seconal, enough to stop a Mack truck. We don't know if he got them from one of his visitors or another inmate or if he was hoarding them somehow." He scowled. "Searches at Charles Street aren't what they ought to be."

"I guess not," said Tip dryly.

"But why would he kill himself?" Kerry asked. "I mean, no one could have forced him to do it. And as long as he was in jail he was relatively safe."

Wykoff shrugged and did not reply. "We can't answer that question, Kerry," Tip told her. "Greg Harvey lived in a world where life, including his own, was pretty cheap. Maybe he thought it was the easiest way out of a tough situation. Maybe he thought he wouldn't die but would be removed to a hospital for mental health observation. Who knows what he was thinking?"

"He had a history of drug abuse," Wykoff pointed out.

"Still, it doesn't make sense," Kerry insisted. "And another thing. If Baldie came to visit him in the afternoon, why did he come after me in the evening? I mean, if Baldie had convinced Harvey to kill himself, then he would have had no need to come after me, would he?"

Tip nodded. "She's right, Wykoff. Looks like Harvey might have crumpled on his own."

"Yeah, well, your Mr. Baldie didn't help lift his mood, that's for sure," said Wykoff. "And in any case, it puts the cap on the A.G.'s case. No defendant, no trial."

"That's true. But it doesn't necessarily mean Claudio is out of danger, does it?" asked Kerry.

Tip looked at Wykoff and thought for a minute before replying. "I think it probably does, Kerry. I mean, even if Claudio decided to come forward on his own and tell what he had overheard during those nights in the gazebo, he has absolutely no evidence to back him up. He can't even positively identify anyone other than Harvey. And, if Santos didn't know that Harvey was going to be out of the picture when he sent his friends to talk to you last night, he surely knows by now. I think the danger is pretty much over in terms of threats to Claudio and to you. Don't you agree, Stan?"

Stan thought for a minute, looking closely at Tip, before responding. "I think you're probably right. That is," he said to Kerry, "if you and your client don't go poking your heads around where you're not supposed to. You know what I mean, Tip?"

Tip nodded. "I know what you mean."

"And how about your friend?" Wykoff asked. He turned to Kerry. "*You* know what I mean, Miss Sullivan?"

Kerry looked at Tip. She was ready to say that she did not know what he meant, but something in Tip's expression made her nod her head. "I understand, Detective Wykoff."

As soon as she had spoken Tip rose. "Well, Stan, thanks for giving us your time and explaining everything to us. I'm sorry things had to end this way."

"So am I," said Detective Wykoff.

"Miss Sullivan will go see her client and let him know what's happened."

"I'm sure your friends at the A.G.'s office have already done that," Wykoff said. "But you might make sure he . . . understands the situation, too."

"Of course." Tip took Kerry's arm and guided her out. It wasn't until they were down the street and in his car that he and Kerry spoke.

"What was that all about?" Kerry asked him.

"That was Wykoff's way of telling us that we should keep our noses clean. Obviously he's going to continue investigating this whole mess, and I guess he doesn't want you or me or Claudio gumming up the works."

Kerry was silent for a moment while Tip pulled the car out into traffic. "I don't see how we could," she said carefully. "I mean, unless we know something he doesn't know, right?"

"Exactly right." Tip kept his eyes trained on the traffic, but Kerry knew that he, too, was being careful. They drove for several blocks in silence. Then Tip suddenly pulled the car over to the side of the road on a quiet one-way street off Beacon Hill. He turned to face her and his expression was serious. "Kerry, I know there's something you haven't told me yet, and I just want you to know that you can trust me with everything."

Kerry feigned innocent surprise. "But Tip, I do trust you. Really I do."

He appeared unmoved. "Everything," he repeated sternly. "I'm not sure why you're leaving something out, but I have the feeling that until you get it off your chest this whole affair won't be over."

"Tip, I promise you, there's nothing that I haven't told you. You know all the facts I do."

"Dammit!" He slammed his hand on the steering wheel so hard that Kerry jumped. "Don't you understand what's at stake here? I'm not just talking about this damned case. I'm talking about you and me, and about our future together. We've both put ourselves in deep, hot water over this case, Kerry—changed our lives dramatically. I refuse to have it hanging over our heads like some elusive ghost, haunting you and keeping you from giving a hundred percent to me." Seeing Kerry staring stiffly out the window, he softened his voice. "Kerry, darling, listen to me. I know you already. I know you so well it almost takes my breath away. Looking at you, is like looking at the part of myself I've been missing for so long in my life. And I refuse to let whatever it is that's bothering you come between us. You have some intuition, some second sense about this thing—I can see it in your face. And you can't hide it from me anymore than you can hide it from yourself."

She turned to him and her expression betrayed immediately that he was right. "Tip, it's really not anything," she said, trying to smile beneath her fear. "It's just a feeling I have, and it's probably nonsense."

"You know it's not," he said in a low voice. "You know you're right. You're just afraid to prove it to yourself." She said nothing, merely widened her eyes and nodded. It had never occurred to her that Tip could delve so deeply into what she herself barely knew was there. "Prove it, Kerry," he said now. "Prove it to yourself, and prove it to me."

She stared at him for a long time before speaking. "Let's go to Claudio's," she said at last. "Claudio will tell me if I was right."

Claudio met them in the tiny kitchen of his mother's house in the North End. He looked a lot stronger than he had at the preliminary hearing the day before and a lot more at ease; apparently the A.G.'s office had already told him about Greg Harvey's death. Although Tip was clearly anxious, he sat quietly and let Kerry do all the talking.

She explained briefly to Claudio that, since the defendant was dead, the case was moot and there was no need for him to testify. She also told him that their civil suit was also null and void since there was no longer anyone to sue, unless Claudio wished to sue Greg Harvey's estate, which she did not advise. Then she told him what had happened to her the night before and why.

"Claudio," she said carefully. "Mr. Sullivan and I are pretty certain that you're out of danger now. And the police feel the same way."

"So do the people at Mr. Sullivan's office," said Claudio. "They don't seem to want much more to do with me now that I can't serve as a witness for them anymore."

Tip smiled dryly. "Of course not, Mr. Partero. Why should they? After all, you don't know anything they don't know, do you?"

Both Tip and Kerry were watching Claudio closely and both saw him blink his eyes and miss a beat before answering. "No," he said. "I don't know anything."

Kerry leaned forward. "Claudio, listen carefully to me. Last night, when I was leaving...when I was walking away from that limousine, I thought I recognized one of the men in it. Not right away, but...well, he looked familiar. And then I remembered something you once told me, or started to tell me, about where those men met other than the gazebo."

Claudio's eyes were hooded. "I don't think I remember telling you anything about that, Miss Sullivan."

"You also mentioned a name to me, Claudio," she went on, ignoring his denial. "You only mentioned it once, and I didn't make any connections then, but I think you did. I think you know the name of this man, and who he is, and I think you know that he meets on a regular basis with Mr. Santos and his friends to exchange information." She paused and straightened in her chair. It was very important that she say this right. "Claudio, I know you feel you're only putting yourself in more unnecessary danger by even talking about this, but I assure you it's too important to forget about. I know we've been through a lot together and it seems now as if everything is over with, and you'd just like to get healed and get on with your life again. But please, if you know anything or think you might know anything about this, please, tell me now."

Kerry was looking directly at the musician, hoping to be able to will him to cooperate by the power in her voice and gaze. She saw him open his mouth to speak and then shut it, looking briefly at Tip and then casting his eyes downward, as if embarrassed.

"It's okay about Tip," she said softly. "He is no longer connected with the A.G.'s office on his matter. I can vouch for his loyalties. You don't have to worry about that."

"Wait a minute," Tip interrupted. "What does the A.G.'s office have to do with anything? Why should it matter if I'm connected with—'' he stopped abruptly and his eyes narrowed. "Kerry," he said tightly after a moment of rigid silence, "I think you had better tell me what's going on."

"I'd like to let Claudio tell you," she said evenly. "Claudio?"

Claudio took a long time to respond, and when he did it was in a small voice, without looking up. "I did hear a name mentioned," he said softly. "I heard it several times. Once Harvey said to someone that when this person met with Santos everything had to be settled or there'd be hell to pay. Another time someone said to Harvey that he had been with this person and Santos at . . . at the beach house, and that was how he knew for certain about something or other. And once Harvey told a guy to wait until the next meeting with Santos and this man, because that was when the guy would get his. You know, a couple of things like that. I didn't get the whole stories, but I got the names."

"You heard this man's name several times, then, didn't you Claudio? And you heard the beach house mentioned, too."

"Yeah, but I already told you about the beach house, Miss Sullivan."

"I know, Claudio. It wasn't until today that I began to connect what happened to me last night with what you told me. And then the name of the man whose face I saw came back to me, too."

"For God's sake," Tip exploded, his voice stricken. "Will one of you please tell me who this mystery man is?"

"Tell him, Claudio. Tell Mr. Sullivan the name you heard mentioned at least three times in the connection with Mr. Santos and these beach house meetings.''

Claudio turned his head slowly to face Tip, but when he spoke his voice was strong. "The man's name was Jason Cromack, Mr. Sullivan. The assistant attorney general."

"I still can't believe it. I just can't believe Jason would be involved in all this."

They were sitting in Tip's car hours later, looking out at the curving stretch of road which bordered Carson Beach. Rush hour traffic was heavy, but the day was overcast and gray and there were very few people on the beach itself. It was just after twilight, and they had been sitting and talking for a long time.

"I know it's hard to believe," Kerry replied, for what was probably the tenth time. "I couldn't believe it myself, when the connection finally dawned on me. As a matter of fact, I didn't even think about it when Claudio first mentioned the name—or mumbled it is more like it."

"When did you put it all together?" Tip asked her, even though he had already heard this story several times as well.

Kerry knew she had to be patient. After all, it wasn't every day that a close friend and mentor was discovered to be working with the opposition. "It wasn't until this morning, when I was telling Detective Wykoff what I had told you last night. I guess last night I was still too shocked to put it together, but something kept nagging at me, sticking in my craw, every time I remembered that last image of the man sitting in the limousine. I knew there was something familiar about him but since I had no idea who Santos was, I figured it was just my mind playing tricks on me."

"You think Santos was in the car?"

"I think he was there with Cromack. I've met Jason Cromack once or twice and seen him on the news occasionally. He has a very distinctive profile, as you know."

"And a very distinctive name, too," Tip remarked glumly.

Kerry nodded. "I guess when I heard Claudio mention Cromack's name I figured it must be another Cromack. Or, to put it more reasonably, it just never occurred to me that it could possibly be *that* Cromack. Then, this morning, when my mental picture was still nagging me, it began to fall into place. I resisted it, of course. But then, when Wykoff said that Baldie could easily be someone's grandfather, something clicked. I mean, if someone's dear old gramps could be a strongman, then why couldn't someone's boss be involved?"

Tip let out his breath in a heavy sigh. "Well, it explains a lot of things—like how anybody besides you and me found out about Claudio's planned testimony before the A.G.'s office ever got hold of him. And it explains why we never seemed to be able to be at the gazebo when anything big was going down; of course, Jason must have seen to that. I wonder how deep he's in it?"

"Maybe he's just trading information so he can crack some really big cases," offered Kerry sympathetically.

Tip scowled. "Nice try, but no chance. This is one of the biggest cases we've had in a while, and it's the one we've had the most trouble cracking. Besides, even if that was what Jason had been up to, it's strictly illegal." He snorted disgustedly. "I always wondered how that guy managed to live so high on the hog. Family money, I figured. Well, I was right—I just had the wrong family."

"Now listen, Tip, let's not jump to any conclusions. We've got to find out more information before we make any judgments. Remember, innocent until proven guilty?"

He looked at her and smiled weakly. Kerry felt a tug of pity for him, he looked so drawn and tortured. "My Kerry," he whispered, shaking his head sadly. "What a mess you've found yourself in, huh? All your idealism about justice for all has really taken a beating, hasn't it?"

She reached out and stroked his hair. "Look who's talking," she chided gently. "The original Dudley Doright. This is hard for you, too, buddy. Don't kid yourself."

"You're right." He turned and looked back out the window. "The thing that really kills me is that I'm powerless to do anything about it. I've already handed in my letter resigning from the case and given my reasons why. Anything I say now will be strictly off the record—not that they'd believe me anyway. And to top it off, guess whose desk got my letter?"

"You mean . . ?"

"Right again. None other than my good buddy, Jason."

"Look, Tip, there must be some way, something we can do to get some hard evidence on Cromack. Why don't we go talk to Tom? He usually has good ideas."

"No! Not Tom. I've already dragged you through the mud on this one, and I won't have my father stuck in it, too. I'll figure something out, but on my own."

They were both silent for a few moments, watching the traffic thin out as night fell across the harbor. Kerry had no intention of letting Tip operate on his own. And she had an idea, but she wasn't sure Tip was ready to hear it.

"Tip, there is something we can do."

"What?"

She took a deep breath. "We can go over to the beach house and see if we can spot the limo again. I mean, if we can get a good look and see for sure that it is Cromack...."

"Nothing doing," he said firmly. "First of all, I refuse to subject you to that sort of danger again. I'm taking you home, Miss Sullivan, and you're going to stay put while I work something out—but without your help, thank you."

"Oh, no you don't," Kerry replied, just as firmly. "If you think I'm going to sit around and wait while you snoop around, you've got another think coming. I'm as involved in this as you are, Tip Sullivan. Even more involved, if you really want to measure." Her voice rose as her annoyance grew. "And I refuse..."

She stopped when she saw that he was smiling at her. "All right, all right, back off." He shook his head, chuckling. "I wasn't really planning on dumping you, Sherlock. I just wanted to give you a chance to back out on your own."

"Oh. Well." Kerry needed a moment to readjust to this bit of news. Then she smiled coyly. "As long as I get to be Sherlock to your Watson, it's all right."

For the first time in hours, Tip really smiled. "Who says I'm Watson? I'm Mike Hammer!" And he reached across to the glove compartment and snapped it open, revealing a small tape recorder with a built-in microphone. "Or maybe I'm James Bond. He's always prepared with the latest gadgets, isn't he? I can't decide...."

"All right, 007, you can be whatever you want to be. But let's get going before I turn into Chicken Little and run to tell the king that the sky is falling."

They got out of the car and began the long walk down the causeway that led to the beach house. It was fully dark now, and drizzling on the deserted beach. There was no sign of activity from the beach house, and the street on either side was deserted as well.

Kerry and Tip secreted themselves into a clump of low bushes just to the right of the beach house, a short way out onto the sand. "They might not come around tonight, of course," Kerry whispered. "I mean, they were here last night, and I doubt Cromack makes this a nightly habit."

"You're probably right," whispered Tip. "On the other hand, there's been big doings today, what with Harvey's death and the police investigation. I doubt they would communicate by phone, so this may be the only chance they'll get to discuss current events." He moved closer to Kerry and dropped a kiss on the back of her neck. "In any case, I'm prepared to wait right here, even if it takes days. Weeks, even."

"Hey. I'm sure Sherlock never made out while he was on a stakeout," Kerry said, responding nevertheless by offering more of her neck to his lips.

"That's because he had stuffy old Watson along. Unlike Mr. Bond, who always had a beautiful blonde at his—Hey, what's that?"

They both froze as a long dark car slid up to the curb directly in front of them. Kerry hadn't realized how close they would be to the car when it pulled up alongside the beach house, and her heart began to hammer loudly against her rib cage.

"My God," she breathed. "They really came."

"Shhh. This mike picks up everything for fifty feet. Let's hope they open their windows, or we're out of luck."

They both peered through the bushes and tried to see inside the car. The interior was dark, but suddenly the door on the street side opened briefly and the occupants were illuminated. Kerry bit back a cry. She could see Baldie clearly silhouetted on the passenger side in the front. In the back were two men. One she did not recognize, but the other was the same man she had seen in the car the previous night. She turned to Tip, although she did not need to ask if the man was indeed Assistant Attorney General Jason Cromack. His face told it all.

One of the windows must have been open, because snatches of conversation drifted back to them. Both Kerry and Tip held their breath, the better to hear what was being said.

"I guess that takes care of that, then," said a deep voice from within the car.

"Yeah, Harvey'll never know what a big favor he did for us, will he?"

"What about it, Eddie? You think they'll be able to pin a positive ID on you from the prison visit?"

"I don't think so," replied Eddie, the bald man in the front seat. "And even if they do, what can they say? I didn't kill the poor jerk. I just scared him a little. They can't even trace the damn pills to me."

"Good. Now, what about the fiddle player?"

"Yes," said the first voice, the deep one. "I am still a bit nervous about the violinist. If he overheard anything that could tie me in with you, Santos, you know what it could mean."

"I know, Mr. C. But you said his lady lawyer friend didn't seem to know about you. Your guy in the office..."

"You mean Sullivan?"

"Yeah, Sullivan. Didn't he say only that the musician had heard there were more guys involved? He would'a called your number if he had heard about you. Don't worry. Besides, he's off the case, and we got to the lady lawyer, so I don't think—"

"It's not a matter of thinking, Mr. Santos," Cromack said coldly. "It's a matter of knowing. You have ways of protecting yourself that I cannot take advantage of."

"Hey, I said not to worry, eh? And I meant not to worry. It's taken care of, believe me."

Tip looked back at Kerry, who shrugged, as if to say she had no idea what that could mean. But something happened when she tried to lower her shoulders. Something was holding them up. It took her an instant to figure out that what was holding them was a hand, hard and unyielding, wrapped around her collarbone.

Tip saw it too, and lunged forward to tackle the assailant. But a small pistol was thrust in his face, and then pulled against Kerry's temple. She and Tip both froze.

"That's a good idea," Bobby said. "If I were you I'd just back right off there, Mr. Hero. Now stand up and walk to the car. I've got somebody who wants to talk to you, real bad."

Chapter Eleven

The fear that Kerry had felt on the previous night was nothing compared to the panic that gripped her now as she was led roughly toward the limousine. For the first time, she felt her life was in real and immediate danger, and the gun at her back made it impossible to conceive of any possible avenue of escape. It was no longer a question of making threats. These man had every intention, and plenty of reason, according to their own sick code, to do away with her permanently. The long black car sat like a sleek menace before her, and Kerry had to resist the impulse to scream from the sheer weight of her predicament.

Then she felt Tip's hand slip briefly into hers and give a reassuring squeeze. Although she had no doubt that he was as helpless as she, the warm pressure gave her strength so that she no longer felt that her legs might give out from under her. The short walk seemed endless.

"Oh, Tip," she moaned softly, keeping her eyes fixed on the looming black shadow alongside the building as if she could will the car away.

"I know, sweetheart, I know." Tip's voice was level and betrayed very little fear, although a quick glance sideways proved that he was very tense. His brow was drawn taut over his eyes and his jaw set in a firm line of concentration. Kerry felt her eyes filling with tears at the sight of him. She had only just found him, and now there was the very real possibility that they would lose each other forever.

Just then he turned to her and smiled. "Would it help at all if I told you not to worry?" he asked lightly.

Kerry's mouth fell open. "Are you kidding?" His blasé attitude may have been intended to assuage her fears but in reality it only made her feel more desolate. Was she the only one who recognized the extent of their danger? "It would not," she said, her voice constricted with pain. "It doesn't help at all."

"Nothing will help right now," he replied, his eyes fixed once again on the darkness ahead. "But don't despair my love. Just don't despair." And he squeezed her hand again.

"Shut up, you two," Bobby muttered from behind them. "This is no time for love talk."

They had almost reached the car, and its occupants had turned to watch their approach. Jason Cromack appeared surprised by their presence, and did a double take when he recognized Tip, but the man who must have been Santos only grinned.

"See, now, Mr. C? I told you there'd be nothing to worry about."

Both Cromack and Santos got out of the car, and Baldie slid out of the front seat to take up a position next to Bobby and behind Tip and Kerry. Flanked as they were on both sides by strong men, Kerry realized that they couldn't have made a run for it even if the gun had not been such a commanding presence at her back. It was obvious to her that Baldie's grandfatherly image was deceptive. Both he and Bobby looked very strong and threatening. And they were well enough concealed by the brick beach house and the surrounding shrubbery that the chances of their being spotted from the street were slim.

She took another quick glance at Tip, who was standing very still in front of Jason Cromack. He appeared to be entertaining no thoughts of escape, but drew himself up to his full height and arched his eyebrows condescendingly at his colleague. "Well, well, Jason. I didn't know you frequented this sort of after-hours joint. You know, you'd better be careful, old boy. This sort of slumming is no good at all for your reputation."

Santos made a move as if to strike Tip, and Kerry gasped, but Jason raised his hand and Santos subsided. "I rather think it's going to be your career that will suffer from this little encounter, Tip. Yours, and your lady lawyer friend's, too."

"Well, we can take it," Tip replied genially. "After all, we haven't invested nearly as much in our reputations as you have in yours. I think there's something positively Faustian about you, Cromack, selling your soul like this. Wonder why I didn't see it before?"

Jason allowed himself a slight sneer. "Perhaps you weren't quite the crackerjack attorney you thought you were."

"Could be." Tip shrugged. "Or it could be that it just never occurred to me to look so deep in the mud for my co-worker's scruples."

This time Tip was grabbed by Bobbie from behind and given a wrenching shove that would have sent a weaker man sprawling. But somehow Tip managed to stay on his feet and even to keep his unwavering gaze on Jason, who actually moved his eyes away to avoid that glittering stare. He looked at Kerry, but she was too busy watching Tip in amazement to notice. She couldn't believe that Tip was grandstanding so obviously and so uselessly in front of these men. Didn't he know that he was only putting them in more danger by aggravating the situation? Or was he so certain that all was lost that he no longer cared about the consequences of his actions? Either way, the prognosis was dismal, and Kerry felt a pit open in the bottom of her stomach. What little hope she had was connected with Tip, and it was draining away fast.

"Your scruples won't do you any good out here, Sullivan," snapped Jason. "If I were you I'd start praying for a little mercy instead of standing there bragging like some Canadian Mountie. You've gotten yourself and your friend in deep hot water, you know."

"So I see," Tip said, looking around and nodding cordially to Santos, as if seeing him for the first time. "Well, the least you can do is introduce us to your circle of friends. I mean, if we're going to be spending some time together, we should get acquainted, right?''

"Tip!" Kerry could not resist crying out his name, and he flashed her a brief look that was so full of empathy and encouragement that she got confused. "Tip," she repeated more softly. "Please be careful."

"Yeah, Miss Sullivan, that's some damned good advice. You tell your friend to watch his mouth before he loses his face." This came from Baldie, behind her, and he spoke in the same soft voice that had chilled her so badly before. Tip turned a brief, incendiary gaze on Baldie but did not say a word.

"I think you know who everybody is," Jason Cromack said in a tightly controlled voice. "Mr. Santos, Mr. Rivera and—" indicating Baldie with a nod of his head "—Mr. McClellan."

"Aka Mr. Richard Harrington, I presume?" Tip inquired. "I was wondering, Mr. Harrington-McClellan, exactly what did you say to Greg Harvey last night to leave him in such an upbeat condition?"

"I told him he won the lottery," Baldie replied sweetly and Bobby Rivera snickered. Kerry shuddered at their callousness.

"And I assume, Jason, that it was your friend Mr. Santos who saw to it that our stakeout on the Common led to a brick wall, so to speak—with your gentle advice, of course."

"You can figure it out for yourself, Sullivan," Jason snapped. "I'm not going to sit here and tell you pretty stories."

"Oh, but you already did. A very pretty story indeed. What I can't figure out is what you traded for. I mean, did you give Mr. Santos privileged information in exchange for a cut of the action? Tell him what busts to avoid and which men to sacrifice—like Mr. Harvey—in order to keep things moving in the A.G.'s office?''

Jason simply stared at him with a stony look of contempt. But Tip was not to be stopped. ''And more to the point, why on earth did you bother? I mean, God knows the state's pay scale is nothing to write home about, but even with your rich tastes you should have been able to manage for the time being. After all, you could have made it to the top, to attorney general, and we all know the sky's the limit after that for an ambitious man like yourself.''

Jason sneered. ''Do we really all know that, Sullivan? Or do we really all know the truth? That I would never have made it to the top on my own, without some extra help from somewhere. And I sure as hell wasn't going to get it from my esteemed colleagues, now was I? Not when half of them would as soon cut my throat as shake my hand. And the other half, or should I say the other privileged few, like you, Tip Sullivan, were obviously going to be shoehorned in ahead of me anyway. You, with your impeccable Irish connections, your Harvard Law degree, your law review articles and your enviable conviction record. An outsider like me didn't have a chance in that office, and you know it.''

The venom that accompanied this seemed to surprise even Jason's own men, for they looked at him with new interest and paid no attention to their captives. ''Perhaps you're right,'' Tip said with something very close to pity in his voice. ''But that's no reason to hook yourself up with these lowlifes, Jason. You should know better than that. These guys are the absolute scum of the earth.''

At that point both Bobby and Baldie jumped Tip. Kerry screamed and reached out for him, but he yelled at her.

"Run, Kerry. For God's sake, run!"

For a brief moment, it seemed as if she could get away. The two strong men were engaged in holding Tip down as he put up a furious struggle, and Santos, who was a short and obese man with a cigar hanging out of his mouth, probably could not have caught her. Jason Cromack might have taken off after her, but somehow Kerry couldn't imagine him, in his three-piece suit and tight collar, running down the street after a young woman. She was probably wrong, but she thought she could get away.

Still, she did not move. Something stopped her, and it wasn't fear—she had gone past fear long ago. By the time she looked around wildly a second time, Santos had grabbed her arm, making it impossible to move because of the sheer mass of his weight holding her back.

It was Tip, of course, who stopped her. She watched as he fought off two men, both clearly skilled fighters. She saw that he was not winning by any means, but that he was holding his own. His fists moved with swift fury and landed blows on both men's faces before they finally got his arms pinned behind his back. Bobby drew back his arm to strike him square in the solar plexus while Baldie held him, but Jason raised his hand again and stopped him.

"No, wait. I'm not done with him yet."

Tip did not seem to hear him, but was looking at Kerry. "Why didn't you run? What made you stay?"

Kerry didn't know who she was madder at—Tip or herself. "You, you big fool," she retorted, irrational fury momentarily overcoming her fear. "I stayed because of you!"

He smiled and shook his head. "You're a dope, you know that?" he inquired tenderly.

"You're a bigger dope!" she snapped, not caring that all four men were staring at her as if she were out of her mind. "Standing here mouthing off while these guys decide when and where they're going to kill us? How can you? How can you be so... so callous?"

But Tip was still smiling tenderly at her. "I'm not being callous, my love. I happen to know that my old friend Jason Cromack can't kill us—not until he finds the tape I left out there, recording every word of this conversation. Jason knows quite well that self-incriminating evidence is particularly hard to refute, don't you, Jason?"

At last Jason Cromack's reserve broke and he grabbed Tip by the shoulders. Jason was taller, but Tip was clearly the stronger of the two. "What tape?"

Tip lifted both hands and pressed them down on Jason's forearms, forcing him to relinquish his grasp. "Oh, come now, Jason. You don't seriously think I would put myself in this kind of situation without backup, do you? I'm a better attorney than that, at least."

"Where's the machine, Sullivan?" Jason asked through clenched teeth. "Violence is not my style, but my associates have no such compunctions." He nodded and Bobby stepped closer to Tip, pressing the gun against his head. "Where did you stash the machine?"

"I threw it when I felt Mr. Rivera coming up behind me," said Tip. "It must be somewhere out there between the bushes and the sand."

Jason gave another signal, and Santos reached forward to take Bobby's gun. "You two go look for that thing," Santos said to his two henchmen. "Find it."

"It's quite small," Tip offered helpfully over his shoulder. "And I suppose I should tell you that I was a star outfielder at prep school. I've got a pretty good arm."

"Shut up," snapped Jason, and Santos trained the gun on Tip. Kerry took a step closer to Tip, although she could not take her eyes off the menacing presence of the small .38 in Santos's hand. She had never seen a gun at such close range before, and had certainly never seen one trained on anybody she knew. Mesmerized by the cold gray steel, Kerry welcomed Tip's comforting arm around her shoulder.

"Still mad at me?" Tip asked.

Kerry shook her head and swallowed. "Just scared," she whispered hoarsely. He did not reply, but squeezed her shoulder in firm reassurance. This time, the gesture helped, and Kerry realized that Tip's bravado had had a positive effect. Their assailants were now off their guard and split into two groups; the two weaker men were with them while Baldie and Bobby were searching for the tape.

Still, the gun was an unassailable reality, and Kerry stared at it as if it were alive. So she did not see Tip turn his head, apparently to watch the search, nor hear the other two men react to the sounds of movement in the bushes. "Gee," Tip said. "I think they're way off in the wrong direction."

Jason and Santos both looked out into the darkness to see what was happening. At that moment Tip lunged forward, pushing Kerry out of the way and ramming up against Santos's bulk. Santos was not easily budged, but his attention had been diverted by the noise in the bushes and Tip's remark, and the gun flew out of his hand as Tip's body slammed into his. Kerry saw what had happened and reacted instantaneously by bending down to pick up the gun. But Jason Cromack was faster than she was and scooped it out from under her fingers as they scrabbled through the sandy soil.

Fortunately Tip was faster than both of them. Pushing Santos rudely aside, he dove beneath Jason's hands. For a moment they struggled, and Kerry staggered back, stumbling into Santos. Santos grabbed her and yanked her arms cruelly behind her back while the two men on the ground battled for possession of the gun. It was more a battle of wills than of bodies—neither man went sprawling to the ground, but their bodies were taut with the force of their concentration. From where she stood, Kerry could not see the outcome of the struggle, and could only wait, wincing in pain and holding her breath, while the ground beneath her feet seemed to vibrate with the men's energy.

At last they straightened, slowly and in unison. Kerry sucked in her breath, and she could hear Santos doing the same behind her. Who had the gun? In the darkness, it was impossible to tell.

Then Tip brought his hand forward and smiled. "Tell your pal to let Kerry go," he whispered, pointing the muzzle of the .38 directly at his former associate. Jason did not even look at Santos. He merely nodded and Kerry felt her arms drop to her sides. She ran over to Tip but did not touch him. For one thing, the gun in his hand still represented a very real threat to her, even though Tip held it. And also it seemed to her she was seeing another dimension of Tip. He was no longer the warm, sparkling companion she knew, but a hard, cold functionary whose entire being was now focused on the action at hand. It was comforting to know that he was on her side but a little frightening to think that he could be so different from the man she thought she knew. Everyone, she was aware, had the capacity for violence. She had just never seen it at such close range in someone she loved.

At that moment all of them became aware that something was going on in the bushes, and Kerry with her heart still in her mouth, turned toward the sound of voices coming through the dark. If Baldie or Bobby had another gun the danger might not yet be over. Tip, of course, had the ace in his hand, but there was no telling what the return of the two other men might do to the balance of power.

As she peered through the night, it took Kerry a moment to realize that there were more than two figures coming toward them. Two men walked in front, followed by two more close behind them, and then, at a short distance, there were another two or three—she couldn't tell. The first group of men stepped into the dim circle of light thrown by the still open door of the limousine. It was Bobby and Baldie, being led by two uniformed police officers.

"Officer Rand, Sergeant Kiley, good to see you." Tip didn't seem in the least bit surprised to find Santos's men under police guard, and in a moment, Kerry saw why. The second group of men emerged from the shadows, and she let out a cry of disbelief.

"Hi, Pop," Tip said, turning to smile at Kerry as he spoke. Kerry was not able to find her voice. "Kerry, aren't you going to say good evening to old Tom?"

"Tom! What on earth..?"

"Evening, Kathleen, Son." Tom stepped into the light and clapped a brief hand on his son's shoulder. Then he turned and clasped Kerry close to his chest, wrapping her in a warm and comforting bear hug. "You all right, my dear?"

"I'm fine.... But what are you...how did you..?" She looked over Tom's shoulder and saw Detective Wykoff standing there. "You, too?"

Stan Wykoff came as close to smiling as he ever did. "Me too. You didn't think the Sullivan family would do this without an audience, did you?"

Kerry turned to Tip, who had handed the gun and Jason Cromack over to Wykoff. "Tip, how did this come about?"

Tip was grinning from ear to ear. "Honestly, Kerry. Did you actually buy that malarky about me not wanting to get my father involved in this scam? Do you really think I would jeopardize your safety before his?"

"Hell, no," Tom said, breaking his own rule about polite language in front of women. "That's my Tip.

Puts his father's neck on the line every chance he gets."

"But when did you get in touch with him? And what...?"

Tip shrugged. "You couldn't very well be with me every moment of the day, could you? A man's entitled to a little privacy, and I made use of mine to call Tom and make arrangements to watch the beach house. We had the whole thing worked out. Then later, in the car, when *you* suggested we watch the beach house—well, I just thought, great minds think alike, don't they?" He narrowed his eyes at Kerry. "Of course, when I tried to get you to run so that some of them would separate and take off after you so Pop could handle his end of the bargain, you refused to leave my side."

"But I didn't know!"

He reached out and drew her from his father's arms into his. "That's okay sweetheart. You made me feel so good that it was worth it."

"It most certainly was not!" Tom declared. "There we were, waiting patiently in the bushes and Pocahontas here refused to leave her captain's side. I nearly fired you on the spot, young lady!"

Kerry broke into a grin, as much from relief as from good humor. She had never been so glad to see anyone as she was to see Tom, but she could not bring herself to leave Tip's side again. And she was glad she hadn't, because he pulled her closer against him and kissed her softly on the hair, lips, eyes—everywhere he could find the space.

"God," he groaned between kisses. "Now that it's over I'm finally beginning to get really scared. What could have happened to you ...!"

"What about you?" Kerry reminded him, nuzzling deeper beneath his chin.

"What happened to me happened on your account," he reminded her, directing her lips to the spot where Bobby had landed a particularly forceful blow. "Next time I say 'run,' will you please run?"

Kerry shook her head. "Uh-uh."

Tip pulled away. "You won't? Why not?"

She smiled up into his eyes. "Not unless you give me a very good explanation first."

Tip laughed and then buried her lips in his, while Tom clucked noisily behind then. "Lady lawyers," he complained to whoever happened to be listening. "I don't know why I ever got involved with a lady lawyer."

"Somehow," Stan Wykoff said, watching Tom as he fondly watched his son kissing Kerry, "I believe you knew why all along."

Chapter Twelve

As it turned out, the case against Jason Cromack, Albert Santos and company was not as strong as the Sullivans would have liked. For one thing, Tip's tape recording of their incriminating conversation in the limousine was inadmissible as evidence in court.

"Of course you must have known that it would be," Kerry pointed out to him. They were sitting in the offices of Sullivan and Sullivan a week later and had left the door ajar so that they could bask in the delightful crisp air of an early fall, which seemed to have arrived just when Bostonians were beginning to feel they had reached their ultimate limit with the summer heat. New England weather had a way of redeeming itself like that.

"There was no way you could have gotten the court to allow that recording to be heard. It was obtained without the proper authority. And anyway, none of the voices on it can be positively identified from so far away,'' she added.

''I knew that,'' Tip told her with a shrug. ''To tell you the truth, I didn't expect the tape to survive our encounter with Santos's thugs at all. I was sure one of those gorillas would step on it or something. It was mostly used as a bargaining tactic, and to gain myself a little time to figure out how in the world I was going to get those guys to separate before they blew our heads off.'' He smiled disingenuously when Kerry shuddered.

''I thought you said there was no chance they would kill us,'' she said, pressing her palm to her chest in an effort to calm her thudding heart.

Tip winked. ''Another diversionary maneuver, I guess.''

''Oh, terrific. You mean we could have been killed?''

He shrugged again. ''I don't know, Kerry. I couldn't gauge Cromack at all, and that was what scared me the most. I mean, he should have known better than to let me pull the tape recorder ploy on him—he has a legal mind like a steel trap.'' He shook his head. ''But I realized that he was not behaving in character at all, at least not in the character of the Jason Cromack I knew. So I must admit, I began to wonder if he really *was* far enough gone to have us killed.''

Kerry shook her head and snorted in disbelief. ''I don't believe it. And there you were, acting so nonchalant, as if we were just play acting in some bad gangster movie. How could you, Tip?''

He reached across the space that separated them and pulled her over onto his chair for a hug. "Just stupid, I guess. Now give me a kiss and make us both feel better."

Kerry was glad to oblige, but the truth was that neither of them needed much help to feel very good indeed. The fact that Cromack, Santos and company weren't likely to get stiff sentences, barely made a dent in their euphoria. Part of their mood stemmed from sheer relief—after all, they were alive, and there had been moments when both of them had been in real fear for their lives.

But part of it was the beckoning pleasures of the future, which the crisp, blue day only seemed to enhance. Everything seemed to be working out right. That morning Tip had gone to a meeting with the attorney general, his first since the hullabaloo over the discovery and arrest of Jason Cromack had died down. Tip had managed to stay on the outskirts of the office upheaval that resulted from Cromack's indictment, although it had been impossible, given his connection with the case, for him to stay out of the public eye. Both he and Kerry had been interviewed numerous times by the press and countless other times by the legal authorities. Both of them felt they had done more than their share and were quite content to let the mechanics of the case go on without them.

But the subject of Tip's letter of resignation had never been discussed until that morning. Tip had come to Kerry's office to let her know how it had gone.

"It was amazing, really," he told her as he began his tale. "To listen to that man talk circles around what happened. He thanked me for my help even though he made it clear that he did not approve of my extracurricular methods. And he condemned Jason's activities even though he made a point of mentioning that he had advanced to assistant A.G. because he was so good at what he did.''

"Sounds like he was trying to play both ends against the middle," Kerry observed. If it had been up to her, Tip would have been honored with a ticker tape parade through the city and immediately elevated to an office no lower than assistant mayor, and maybe even to governor. As for herself, she had never been so grateful to be back at work on Dorchester Avenue. After what she had seen in the past two weeks, she was sure it was the best job in the world.

"The A.G. is a scrupulously fair man," Tip said, always fair himself. "I think he was trying to let me know that nothing is ever black and white and that I shouldn't expect more than my share of credit for this whole thing."

"But that's not fair at all!" Kerry exclaimed.

"Then," Tip added with a grin, "he told me that he was putting my name in for promotion to Cromack's position. He said as far as he was concerned, that letter I wrote does not and never did exist. I'm still on active duty."

Kerry, still perched on his lap, nearly sent them both sprawling with her enthusiastic hug. "Oh, Tip, that's great! That's absolutely wonderful! Of *course* you should be assistant A.G.! You're going to be attorney general someday, aren't you?"

Tip laughed. "Whoa, girl, not so fast." He settled her more firmly against him so that they didn't both spill onto the floor. "I think that's one of the reasons he used the tone he did. Partly to warn me that nothing comes easily in that office, and that too much ambition, as Jason Cromack so brutally proved, is not necessarily a good thing. And he was also pointing out to me that he has no intention of relinquishing his position in the near future.''

"Well," she said, snuggling against him for one last kiss before popping up again and returning to her desk. "Someday, I'm sure."

"Perhaps." Tip's eyes were momentarily far away. "Although to tell you the truth, Ker, sometimes I'm not so sure that's what I'd really want. I mean, that job is so political, and he spends so much of his time wheeling and dealing. I don't think the man has worked personally on a case for years. I mean, really worked and not just come in for the window dressing. And he's as good as they come, believe me." He shook his head. "I'm not so sure I'm cut out for that kind of thing."

"Sure you are!" Kerry looked up from the Stuart file, which lay opened before her on her desk. Her eyes were so full of conviction that Tip had to laugh.

"I guess I'd get used to it pretty quick, huh?" Then he leaned forward in his chair. "And what about you, my love? What are your intentions?"

Kerry sifted through the papers. "First order of business is to get your father to apologize to Elsie Carpenter so I can get this Stuart case finished with. Then...I don't know. Tom'll have something for me, I know. The phone's been ringing off the hook lately." She looked around the shabby office and smiled. "Whatever it is, I'll be grateful for it. I've never been so glad to be anyplace in my life."

"Anyplace?" Tip's eyes lit up with that special smoky glitter that meant he was thinking of the long nights they had been spending together in his bed or hers.

"Well," she replied demurely, "almost anyplace."

"You know," he said after a pause during which they smiled secretly into each other's eyes. "You could move on, Kerry, if you wanted to."

Kerry looked up. "What do you mean?"

He was watching her closely as he replied. "I mean, the A.G. asked me about you. Said he had heard some good things about your work, and wondered if you might be interested in coming over to our office."

"You mean, work there?"

He smiled indulgently. "Kerry, I didn't mean just for a tour of the place. Of course, to work there! No guarantees, you understand, but he did seem pretty interested." Kerry did not reply, but stopped what she was doing and stared out the open front door without seeing anything. An offer to work in the Attorney General's office! It was what she had been dreaming of for so many years, and now here was Tip telling her that the attorney general wanted her! She couldn't have plotted the scenario any better if she had written it herself. They were coming to her, offering her a job that would pull her out of the tacky world of Dorchester Avenue forever! She needed time to let it all sink in.

"And I must admit," Tip added slyly, seeing her bemusement and hoping to add to the enticement, "I'd like to have you there too. To keep an eye on you, of course. See that you don't get into trouble."

Kerry was too absorbed in her own thoughts to rise to this teasing bait, but someone else heard it. "Get into trouble?" Tom inquired, lumbering in and casting a temporary shadow across the dazzling sunlight from outside. "Now what makes you think anyone could get into any trouble around here? This is a nice, quiet neighborhood, Tip, my boy. Unlike that inferno you call downtown Boston."

Both Tip and Kerry started guiltily. Tom had gone out to the Gaelic Pub as soon as Tip had arrived, and neither had expected him back so soon. Kerry hoped that Tom hadn't heard Tip's offer to her. It would break his heart, she thought, if she left Sullivan and Sullivan, too. She still suspected that he might be waiting for his son to rejoin the firm, although now that Tip had been nominated for a big promotion Tom might realize that his son was not planning to return to Dorchester Avenue at all. If she defected to the same camp, she thought, he would really feel alone and rejected. She couldn't bear to see that happen to him.

But Tom appeared to have no such heavy thoughts on his mind. "Kerry," he said, coming over and leaning across her desk. "I've done it."

"Done what, Tom?"

"I've made the supreme sacrifice for you, my dear girl. I actually went and apologized to Elsie, er, to Miss Carpenter. And she's agreed to testify, so you can just go ahead with proceedings. Although I think that old Louise will probably drop the charges when she knows that we've got Elsie in our camp."

"Hey Dad," Tip said with a chuckle, "what'd you have to do to get her to accept your apologies?"

To Kerry's surprise, Tom actually blushed. "Oh, nothing, nothing."

"Come on, Dad," Tip chided.

"Well, so we're going to the Masonic Temple dinner Saturday night," Tom growled unwillingly. "So what? I would have gone anyway."

Tip started to hoot, but both Kerry and Tom cast him such dark warning glances that he subsided immediately.

"Thanks, Tom," Kerry said warmly. "I really appreciate it." She allowed herself a small grin. "I know what a sacrifice it must have been."

"No, you don't," Tom retorted. "You have no idea." Then he brightened. "By the way, Kerry, there was a message for you earlier. That Mr. Partero of yours called this morning while you were out."

"He did? What's wrong?" Claudio Partero had not had to testify much during the preliminary hearing against Santos and Cromack since his testimony was mostly hearsay and thus inadmissible. Still, Kerry felt that she had put him through unnecessary pressure during the course of their professional relationship. She wondered if he ever regretted using that business card she had slipped into his pocket that fateful night.

Tom shook his head. "Nothing's wrong. Nothing at all. He called with good news, as a matter of fact. Said all this publicity had done some good, that he had been approached by the music director of a good chamber group who was interested in hearing him play. Fortunately Partero had some excellent tapes of his work recorded before the shooting, and he says the man was very impressed." He smiled. "He says to tell you you've got complimentary front row seats at his debut performance next month.''

"Next month! That's terrific!" Kerry beamed.

Tom returned to his desk and sat down. "Well, it looks like everyone is finally getting what they want, wouldn't you say, Tip?"

"Looks like it, sir.'' Something in Tom's voice was making Tip uneasy, Kerry thought, and she thought she knew why.

"And what about you, my boy? Have you made any plans to get what you want?"

Tip cleared his throat. "Well, sir, as a matter of fact—"

He broke off, and Kerry blurted, "Tip's being promoted to assistant attorney general, Tom. Isn't that marvelous?"

Her voice was full of forced gaiety, and she was ashamed of herself for having opened her mouth and not letting Tip give his father the news. But somehow, she'd felt she had to soften the blow for both of them. Tip cast her a baleful glance and then faced his father, awaiting the consequences.

"Is that true, son?" Tom asked. His expression was hard to read from under his bushy brows.

"Well, not quite true yet, sir," Tip allowed. "After all, I do have to go through the usual nomination procedure, and there are no guarantees, as I told Kerry." Another glance warned Kerry not to interfere again. "And besides, I'm not sure that's what I want to do with my life. After all, it would mean a pretty long-term commitment to the job, and..."

"Not sure that's what you want to do with your life?" Tom's words exploded from his mouth.

"Thomas P. Sullivan Junior, are you actually sitting there telling me you might be considering turning such an offer *down*?"

Tip looked surprised at his father's vehemence. "Well, not exactly, but I did think . . ."

"What did you think?" Tom demanded.

Tip took a deep breath. "Dad, my name is out there over that door, just like yours. I'm not going to pretend I don't know what it's there for."

Kerry was glad that Tip had decided to confront the matter head-on, but Tom did not seem pleased at all. "Now you listen to me, Tip," he growled. "If I find out that you turned down an offer like the one you got this morning, so help me, I'll take your name off that door before you can say Tip Sullivan. If you think I've worked all my life to see you chuck a chance at the biggest, juiciest job in the state, then you've sadly misjudged me. Sadly misjudged me, my boy."

Tip started to grin. "Why you old . . . ! All this time I thought you'd been waiting for me to come back here, and now you tell me you'll take my name off the door?"

Tom's eyes began to twinkle, although he still scowled. "Take you out of my will, too, for what it's worth. No son of mine is going to turn down a chance at the top just because his name is on a peeling wooden board." He turned to Kerry. "As a matter of fact, I'd disown anyone who refused a chance for advancement on what they think is my account. Why the very idea is enough to turn my stomach!"

So he had heard. Heard, or else he had intuited that she, too, might be leaving him. Kerry felt the power of his gaze and Tip's, and she could not meet either one.

She looked down at the open Stuart file in front of her, staring at the words on the yellow foolscap until they ran together.

"Kerry?" It was Tip's voice, gentle and curious. Kerry took a long time before raising her eyes, but when she did they were shining. The decision was easy to make after all.

"I'm not planning to go anywhere, Tom," she said softly. "As long as you need a Sullivan for that shingle, I'll be here." And she meant it.

There was a brief silence as all three of them let out their breath and smiled at one another. Kerry was sure it was the right decision, and she could tell by Tom's expression that he was glad, although he never would have admitted as much. Tip was the only person she wasn't sure about, even though he seemed to be smiling as broadly as she was.

"I guess that makes sense," Tip said at last. "I don't know of any other law firm in the city that offers such good honeymoon benefits."

"Honeymoon benefits?" At last, Tom looked astounded.

"Maternity benefits, too," Tip went on casually.

"Maternity benefits?" Now it was Kerry's turn to be surprised.

"Well, of course," Tip explained patiently. "Oh, Dad, didn't we tell you? Kerry and I are planning to get married."

"Married, sure," Kerry interjected. "But I don't recall planning any maternity leaves in the near future."

"Not to worry," Tip assured her confidently. "That'll come of it's own accord, believe me. And don't worry about job security while you're out with the babies. I have an in with your boss.''

He had come over to stand behind Kerry's chair, and had placed his hands protectively along her arms, and now both of them faced Tom, waiting for his re-action.

For once Tom appeared to be at a loss for words. But, just when Kerry began to think that his emotions had overtaken him, he broke into a big grin. ''Well, I must say,'' he boomed, ''it's about time! I've been watching you two dancing circles around each other ever since the first moment you met. I mean, I knew that you'd be perfect for each other, but I had no idea—''

''Wait a minute!'' Tip interjected. ''What do you mean, you knew?''

'''Course I knew. I've had this match planned ever since I met our Kathleen here. You think I hired her just because she was a good lawyer?''

''I'd like to think that had something to do with it,'' Kerry remarked dryly.

''It did. Of course it did. But I had other plans for you, my dear. Big plans.''

''Carrying on the Sullivan line, that was your big plan for Kerry?'' Tip inquired, grinning and squeez-ing Kerry's shoulders. ''Dad, I think you've opened yourself up to accusations of sexism there.''

''Well, of course, if she had wanted to move on, to go for the top, I would have supported her, in that case too.'' Tom waved aside Tip's remark. ''But I knew my Kerry. I knew she felt too good about Dorchester Avenue to think about leaving once she got settled here. And besides,'' he added, with a perfectly straight face, "who could resist exciting cases like the Ranieri case?"

All three of them laughed. "Tom," Kerry said fervently, "after the past few weeks, believe me, the Stuart case is starting to look pretty good. And anyway, business is picking up. We've got some fascinating cases coming up—none of them dangerous, I'm happy to say."

"Well that's only natural," Tip said, bending down and sliding his arms around Kerry's neck. "Everyone wants a Sullivan on their side these days."

"That's good, that's good," Tom said, rubbing his hands together in anticipation. "And if I have anything to say about it, there'll soon be plenty of Sullivans to choose from."

Tip and Kerry responded in unison. "You don't."

Things weren't perfect on the Avenue by any means. Marie got into a terrible fight with her boyfriend and had to spend a week hiding at Kerry's until the man calmed down and stopped making outrageous threats in the Gaelic Pub concerning her safety. By the time the danger was passed, Kerry had already moved into Tip's apartment, and Marie had struck up a promising relationship with a telephone sales representative who lived in Kerry's building.

"He's not Dorchester," Marie confided to Kerry one afternoon when they were out shopping for a wedding dress. "But he's a damned sight more gentlemanly than most of the guys I know from the Avenue. And Kerry, he really thinks I'm terrific!"

"That's good news," Kerry laughed. "Although I've always thought you were pretty terrific."

"Yeah," snorted Marie. "But what kind of future could you offer me?" She winked broadly and then, spotting something amid the racks of elegant lace and satin gowns that hung on the rack of the Newbury Street bridal boutique, she reached in and pulled out a cream-colored negligee with a low-cut bodice and sheer lace over the breasts and loins. "Now this," she said, holding the scanty gown over her hips and parading across the thick carpet, "is what I call a wedding dress."

"Marie, that's a nightgown!"

"Yeah, but what's the use of dolling yourself up in all that demure finery when this is what weddings are all about?" She rolled her eyes expressively. "Wear this, and you don't even have to change for the honeymoon."

Other Avenue events did not turn out as well. There was a stabbing on Neponset Boulevard, and a series of robberies. Louise Ranieri's case against Billy Stuart was dropped, but Elsie Carpenter began haunting poor old Tom until he could barely get from his office to the Pub without being intercepted by her relentless pursuit and forced into having lunch at the very proper Roman Gardens restaurant, where Elsie could show off her new catch.

Still, for Tip and Kerry things were as close to perfect as they could be. Kerry's family was planning to come up to Boston for the wedding; Tip had been given the promotion to assistant attorney general, and Kerry was busy with the kind of righteous cases she had always wanted to pursue. Sitting close together on the couch in Tip's apartment, with the cool fall night sparkling across Boston Harbor outside the window, it was hard to think of a single thing wrong with the world.

"I know it's not always going to be this perfect," Kerry murmured, bringing her bare legs up beneath her so that she could move even closer against Tip's warm flank. "I know I'm going to have cases that are going to make me want to run screaming out of that office."

"My father'll probably make you want to run screaming out of the office on occasion."

Kerry giggled. "He's been known to produce that effect. It's nice to see him on the receiving end of it for a change with Elsie Carpenter."

"Hey, who knows? Old Elsie may get him yet." Tip curled his arm over Kerry's shoulder and let his fingers dangle inches away from her bare breast, although he made no move to fondle it. "And don't you forget, my girl. I am my father's son to some extent. There may be times when you want to run screaming out of this apartment, too."

Kerry looked down at his long fingers and at her own nipple, which was hardening in sheer anticipation of his caress. "Oh, I don't know," she murmured, wondering whether it would be more pleasurable to lean forward into his hand, or to wait for him to move and prolong the anticipatory delight. She decided to wait. "You know, there are probably some things about me you won't like either, once you find out about them."

"Like what, for instance?" He moved his fingers fractionally closer and Kerry had to resist the urge to thrust her breast out to meet his fingers. Her entire body was tingling.

"I can't think of anything right now. But it's like...like that night with Cromack and Santos, when you finally had the gun." She turned to look at him, moving carefully so as not to spoil the game.

"Uh-hmmm?" Tip was smiling, but she knew from his face that he was very aware of what was going on with his hand.

Kerry looked deep into his eyes, searching there for a sign of that hard, cold person she had seen holding the gun. She could find no trace. "That was a side of you I had never thought existed. You were so...so brittle, so remote, as if the only thing in the world for you was revenge."

Tip nodded. "I think that was true at the time," he said solemnly. "I know I was trying very hard to control myself. I knew I had the power to kill another man at my disposal, and that's not the kind of power a man can wear comfortably." He cocked his head. "Did that scare you about me?"

Kerry shook her head. "No. It only made me see...how much I still have to learn about you." She smiled slowly. "And it made me very glad that I would have the rest of my life to do it in."

Tip smiled, too. Then his eyes slipped from hers to his hand, dangling beside her erect nipple. "Well, I suggest," he said in a deep, throaty voice, thick with desire, "that we have our next lesson in mutual discovery right now."

Kerry opened her mouth to agree, but all that came out was a sigh of happiness. Contact had been made.

Take 4 Silhouette Special Edition novels
FREE
and preview future books in your home for 15 days!

When you take advantage of this offer, you get 4 Silhouette Special Edition® novels FREE and without obligation. Then you'll also have the opportunity to preview 6 brand-new books —delivered right to your door for a FREE 15-day examination period—as soon as they are published.

When you decide to keep them, you pay just $1.95 each ($2.50 each in Canada) *with no shipping, handling, or other charges of any kind!*

Romance *is* alive, well and flourishing in the moving love stories of Silhouette Special Edition novels. They'll awaken your desires, enliven your senses, and leave you tingling all over with excitement . . . and the first 4 novels are yours to keep. You can cancel at any time.

As an added bonus, you'll also receive a FREE subscription to the Silhouette Books Newsletter as long as you remain a member. Each issue is filled with news on upcoming books, interviews with your favorite authors, even their favorite recipes.

To get your 4 FREE books, fill out and mail the coupon today!

Silhouette Special Edition®

Silhouette Books, 120 Brighton Rd., P.O. Box 5084, Clifton, NJ 07015-5084

Silhouette Special Edition

COMING NEXT MONTH

SOMETHING ABOUT SUMMER—Linda Shaw
State Prosecutor Summer MacLean didn't know what to do when she
found herself handcuffed to a suspect determined to prove he was
innocent . . . and who happened to look like her late husband.

EQUAL SHARES—Sondra Stanford
When Shannon Edwards inherited fifty-one percent of a troubled
business, she went to check it out. She expected a problem, but not the
sexiest man alive . . . her partner.

ALMOST FOREVER—Linda Howard
Max Conroy was buying out the company where Claire worked, and used
her to get the vital information. What he didn't figure on was falling in
love.

MATCHED PAIR—Carole Halston
The handsome gambler and the glamorous sophisticate met across the
blackjack table, and it was passion at first sight. Neither realized they were
living a fantasy that could keep them apart.

SILVER THAW—Natalie Bishop
Mallory owned prize Christmas trees, but had no one to market them. The
only man willing to help her was the man who had once sworn he
loved her.

EMERALD LOVE, SAPPHIRE DREAMS—Monica Barrie
Pres Wyman had been the school nerd. But when Megan Teal hired him to
help her salvage a sunken galleon, she found the erstwhile nerd had
become a living Adonis.

AVAILABLE THIS MONTH:

FOUR UNIQUE SERIES
FOR EVERY WOMAN YOU ARE...

Silhouette Romance

Heartwarming romances that will make you
laugh and cry as they bring you all the wonder
and magic of falling in love.

6 titles
per month

Silhouette Special Edition

Expanded romances written with emotion and
heightened romantic tension to ensure
powerful stories. A rare blend of passion and
dramatic realism.

6 titles
per month

Silhouette Desire

Believable, sensuous, compelling—and
above all, romantic—these stories deliver
the promise of love, the guarantee
of satisfaction.

6 titles
per month

Silhouette Intimate Moments

Love stories that entice; longer, more
sensuous romances filled with adventure,
suspense, glamour and melodrama.

4 titles
per month